Bella

Cursed World

Forbidden Love

THE BELLA SERIES

RICK SANCHEZ

Book Cover by Rick Sanchez

Illustrations by Rick Sanchez

First edition 2025

"From one man's hunger came a thousand nightmares—
and from a single forbidden touch, a hope strong enough to defy them."

Werewolf
Legion

G

mancer
Allies

Ancient Vampire
Colonies

CONTENTS

For my family,
the roots that hold me steady and the light that guides me forward.
To my daughter and my sisters—
my first critics, my fiercest encouragers,
you gave me truth when I needed it
and faith when I faltered.
This book is as much yours as it is mine.

PROLOGUE

THE QUEEN'S REMEMBRANCE

The world still bled from the Reckoning.

To Bella, it had never ended. Every breath carried the taste of ash; every heartbeat dragged her back to the day she had lost him.

Now she ruled from the heart of the Sanctum—upon a throne carved from a single, unyielding Heartstone. No crown adorned her brow, yet she was queen all the same. Her reign was not gilded in ceremony but forged in silence and fear.

A scar traced down her temple, white against skin that had weathered both magic and grief. Her hands, calloused and strong, gripped the throne's cold arms as she gazed through the high window at the moon: pale, merciless, eternal. In its light, she remembered him—the prisoner, the man she had loved. His defiance. His kindness. His death.

The chamber doors groaned open. Two guards dragged in a vampire, young, barely turned, its eyes still holding shards of its humanity. It fought the chains, teeth bared.

Bella's voice was stone.

"The new warding sigil must be tested. Take it east. Shackle it. Let it burn."

The guards obeyed. Screams echoed briefly, then were swallowed by the shutting doors. Bella remained at the window, watching as dawn's light claimed the prisoner. Smoke rose from its chest, then face, then limbs bound behind its back. Ash scattered on the wind.

She did not move. The world expected her to mourn or to rage. Instead, she felt only the emptiness that had long since devoured her. No number of executions could fill it. The callus lay not just on her hands, but in her soul. Vampires, she told herself, deserved nothing less.

Her gaze shifted to the war map spread across the table—three territories carved in blood and betrayal. Broken though the world was, it now belonged to her. And she would not falter.

Yet in the silence, the ghost of a lonely girl still whispered.

Later, during a lesson on sympathetic Geomancy, Bella placed a Heart-stone in a boy's hands. "Imbue it with love," she said.

The boy, grief-stricken, tried. Nothing happened.

Bella took the stone back and crushed it between her fingers. Dust spilled across the floor.

"Love is not fuel for our craft," she told them, her voice low and rough. "Love is a weakness. A beautiful lie. It will kill you. Geomancy is for survival. A weapon. A shield. Nothing more."

The students sat frozen, pale in the torchlight. They had sought wisdom. What they found was a queen of vengeance, a mother of grief, and the architect of a new, merciless order.

And the world would remember her not for mercy, but for the terror she left behind.

CHAPTER ONE

THE CURSED ACOLYTE

THE ANCIENT BOOK

T he world was not remade by gods or divine fury. It was remade by a man.

Faust Modaine was no hero. Pale, slight, balding too young, he was overlooked by all who knew him. Neither handsome nor charming, he passed through his village as a shadow no one cared to see. Spurned by women, ignored by peers, Faust turned to the only companions who would not laugh at him: books.

In their pages, he sought what the world denied him—glory. Recognition. A place in history.

The Storm

In the year of the Great Storm, when rains drowned rivers and mountains slid into valleys, Faust climbed the sodden northern hills. There, outside a cavern half-swallowed by a landslide, he found it: a stone jutting from the mud, square and unnatural. Beneath it lay a book bound in hide he could not name, smelling of damp earth and forgotten graves.

Its pages whispered of power. Not wisdom, not faith—power. The drawings were crude but compelling: stones, animals, strange symbols. He could not read the words, but the images burned into him.

He began to mimic them.

At first, nothing. Weeks of failure, of muttered sounds and awkward gestures. Then—success. A pebble shifted when pressed against a clear quartz. A larger stone rolled. A different mineral sparked a faint glow. He discovered the clearer the stone, the stronger the reaction. And with every success, his hunger grew.

But stones were not enough.

His first living subject was a cave bat. He pressed the spell into its frail body. It convulsed, shrieked, and when it took flight, its eyes glowed blood-red. It vanished into the night—rabid, changed, thirsty. Faust did not hesitate. His curiosity only sharpened.

Next, a wolf pup. The spell blackened its fangs with venomous magic. It lunged at him, eyes burning like coals. Only its youth saved him. Snarling, it fled into the forest.

Within weeks, both beasts had spread their curse. The bat birthed nightmares in the sky. The wolf left villages screaming in blood. Fear spread faster than the rainwater that had birthed his discovery.

Faust did not weep. He exulted.

Consumed

It did not take long for Faust to move from stone to flesh. The first spark of success had been enough to ignite a hunger that could not be quenched. Nights blurred into weeks, his fingers blackened with soot from burnt offerings, his breath ragged from whispered incantations.

The bat had been a test of chance. Its frail body writhed, shrieked, and when it lifted into the cavern air with eyes glowing red, Faust felt triumph rather than pity. He marked every detail: the way its wings beat with unnatural strength, the froth on its lips, the shrill cries that echoed like knives. To him, it was not a creature in torment. It was proof.

Then came the wolf pup. Its small fangs blackened with venom under his hand, its young body convulsing as if the spell itself tore at its marrow. When it lunged at him, snapping with feral fury, Faust laughed. Even as it fled into the forest, leaving trails of broken branches, he wrote furiously in the margins of the book. *The younger the subject, the more pliable the flesh. The curse takes root faster.*

By the month's end, villages whispered of shadows that clawed at rooftops, of animals whose eyes burned like coal. The bat birthed swarms of rabid kin; the pup carved its hunger into livestock and children alike. Fear spread like sickness, but to Faust, each story was a hymn of validation. The old world was crumbling, and it was crumbling *because of him.*

He did not mourn. He did not pray. He only pressed further.

The first human came by chance—a farmer's child taken from a field at dusk, bound beneath a black oak. Faust watched the boy cry until his throat broke raw but felt nothing. His heart had long since calcified into stone. He did not seek the child's death, only the transformation, the moment when flesh surrendered to his will.

When the half-formed wolf-beast circled from the tree line, drawn by the scent of blood, Faust's breath caught—not with fear, but with wonder. The boy's scream fractured into a howl as bones cracked and skin split, his hands curving into claws. He tore through the ropes and vanished into the woods alongside his sire, leaving only shreds of cloth and the stink of new hunger behind.

Faust closed his eyes and smiled.

The book consumed him. What began as pebbles shifting in his palm had become lives rewritten, the innocent sacrificed for knowledge only he could wield. It whispered still, its pages breathing with promises—dominion, legacy, godhood. Each word etched itself into him until he could no longer separate his own thoughts from the voice in the vellum.

And in that hunger, the world itself was devoured.

A New World

From Faust's arrogance, the old world burned.

The first to rise were the vampires. Born of the cursed bat's lineage, they slithered from crypts and ruined chapels, their veins filled with venom that made them eternal. Cities once filled with prayers and merchants became their hunting grounds. Families barred their doors at dusk, yet still shadows slipped through shutters, teeth sinking into throats as softly as a lover's kiss. They nested in castles blackened by fire, their hunger not just for blood but for dominion. Lords of shadow, immortal and merciless, they crowned themselves kings of ash.

Then came the werewolves, carved from the curse of the pup. They ran in savage packs through the forests, howls carrying for miles under the silver gaze of the moon. No palisade nor gate could keep them out. They struck with frenzy, tearing flesh from bone, but worse than their claws was the terror they sowed. Entire villages fled at the sound of distant howling, abandoning homes to the wild, leaving only splintered doors and blood-stained earth behind. To the wolves, weakness was prey, and the night was endless.

And still, humans endured. Fragments of a broken race scattered and desperate, they turned to the very magic that had cursed them. Stones carved with trembling hands became wards against the dark. Blood was bound into sigils, fire traced into circles, prayers whispered not to gods but to the earth itself. From the rubble of shattered kingdoms, they raised enclaves—fragile bastions of hope encircled by runes and sacrifice.

The balance was fragile. Vampires in their ruined halls, werewolves in their wild dominions, humans caged within their own wards—all three powers clawing for survival in a world that no longer belonged to them.

And at the center of it all stood Faust Modaine, no longer a forgotten villager but the architect of ruin. He had not built kingdoms nor armies, but something far greater: a legacy of terror that would outlive him. His name would be etched not in monuments, but in screams, in ash, in the cursed blood of generations yet unborn.

From the hands of one man—overlooked, unwanted, and unworthy—three powers were born. And the world would never be whole again.

CHAPTER TWO

HUMAN MAGIC AND THE ENCLAVES

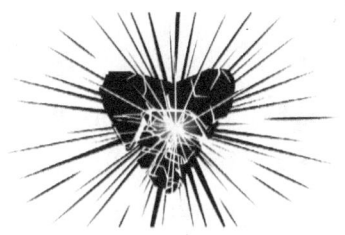

THE PLAN

The magic of humanity was born not of ambition, but of desperation. It was not fire hurled across battlefields or lightning called from the heavens. It was quieter, subtler woven from stone, blood, and survival itself.

At the heart of every enclave stood a Heartstone, a carved altar that drank from the earth's unseen currents. Around it, the Geomancers built their wards: sigils etched into stone, charms strung into necklaces, rings, and amulets. These trinkets were not vanity—they were lifelines. They allowed a mage to stray from the Heartstone's presence and still grasp a fraction of its strength.

Alone, a Geomancer was fragile. But together, bound by sympathetic ritual, they could shatter walls, raise barriers of hardened earth, or strike a monster dead with the weight of the ground beneath its feet.

The Geomancers ruled the enclaves. Their word was law, their philosophy absolute. Emotion was weakness. Love was liability. Order was survival. The walls of their schools echoed with silence, broken only by chants and the scratch of quills on parchment. Here, children were molded into tools of stone and ward, taught that compassion would destroy them, and only control could preserve what remained of humanity.

The Lestaires

Among these children was Bella Lestaire, nineteen years of age. She bore the pale skin of her kin, hair black as the midnight sky, and eyes the color of deep water. Beauty followed her like a curse, stoking envy, desire, and quarrels she never sought. But it was not her beauty that made her dangerous.

It was her heart.

Bella questioned. She felt. Where her peers smothered their emotions under the weight of doctrine, she dared to embrace hers. *To live without feeling,* she believed, *was not to live at all.*

Yet rebellion did not make her weak. Geomancy came to her as naturally as breath. Where others struggled for weeks to stir a pebble, Bella coaxed stone to shift at her touch. Where wards flickered and died for her classmates, hers burned steady and strong. In time, she crafted a breakthrough that secured her enclave's survival: charms cut from the Heartstone itself, worn on chains around the neck. These tokens carried its power beyond the Sanctum's walls, allowing Geomancers to wield their craft in the field.

The elders took notice. They watched her with awe—and with fear. For one so young to hold such power was unnatural. And unnatural things were something to keep at bay.

Her father, Loryndor Lestaire, loved her dearly. Yet his loyalty to the enclave was iron, stronger even than blood.

One morning, he walked Bella to her lessons at the Sanctum. She kissed his cheek, light against the black of his beard, and went inside. As the door closed behind her, a voice rasped from the shadows.

"Loryndor," said Elder Myr Straus, the eldest of the council. His face was a map of wrinkles, his back hunched, but his eyes gleamed sharp as knives. "How goes your day? How fares Bella, since her mother's absence?"

Loryndor sighed. "She smiles, but I see through it. A father knows. She has lost something she will not speak of."

Myr's lips curled in a semblance of sympathy. "A shame. Those vampires—monsters, every one of them. Yet I must speak plainly, Loryndor. Bella's gift... it is too great. For the enclave, the time has come to consider her future."

Loryndor stiffened. "Her future?"

"Marriage," Myr said softly. "An alliance. Elder Franc Boyd's grandson, Jorric. A fine young mage. If your house and his were joined, our strength would be... formidable."

Loryndor frowned. "She must have a say in this."

For the first time, the mask slipped. Myr's voice sharpened. "You are her father. She must do as she is told."

Dangerous Magic

Beyond the wards, humans wove sympathetic magic into every act of survival. Farmers whispered to their fields, binding their hands to soil so harvests would grow heavy. Hunters whispered to their arrows, ensuring each shaft would strike true. Blood from a captured vampire could be carved into sigils that burned their kin on contact. A werewolf's shed fur could be woven into snares that hardened into living cages.

Fragile magic. Desperate magic. And yet it kept humanity alive.

Bella needed no such cruelties. With only the touch of stone and the earth beneath her feet, she could summon strength. The elders watched her carefully, whispering among themselves. For they all saw what Bella did not: that she was not merely gifted. She was too powerful for her own good.

Elder Myr stood in the quiet of the Sanctum corridor, Loryndor's footsteps fading away. The discussion about Bella's future still burned in his chest, but his thoughts drifted back—not to the girl she was now, but to the child she had once been.

He remembered the storm.

The year had been cruel, rain without end, flooding rivers, tearing houses apart. That night, lightning clawed at the sky, thunder rolling through the earth like war drums. Within the Sanctum, the Heartstone chamber shook under the strain of failing wards. The carved runes, usually steady and glowing, flickered like dying embers.

Myr had been younger then, his back straighter, his voice strong as he joined the other elders in their chants. They pressed their palms against the Heartstone, channeling their will to hold the wards together. Sweat dripped into their eyes, and still the runes dimmed. Fear rippled through the chamber—elders feared collapse, and the gathered children, herded for safety, huddled in corners, whimpering as the storm rattled the tower.

And then—silence.

Not outside, where wind still screamed through the night, but within the stone itself. Myr felt the shift before he saw it. A new current, raw and unbidden, surged into the chamber. The tremors stilled. The Heartstone's glow returned, flaring brighter than before.

He turned—and saw her.

Bella, no older than six, stood with her small hands pressed against the floor. Dark hair clung wet to her pale face, eyes wide, unblinking. She whispered something—words no elder taught her, syllables carried like echoes from the earth. The cracks in the floor sealed. The light in the runes steadied. The wards blazed with strength enough to withstand the storm's fury.

The chanting faltered. Elders fell silent, staring at the girl who did not even seem to know what she had done. She looked up at them, innocent, almost afraid of their stares, her blue eyes reflecting the glow of the Heartstone.

Myr remembered the cold that ran through him then. Awe, yes—but also dread. A power that did not belong to a child, or even to the elders themselves. It was instinct, elemental, a connection to the earth that surpassed doctrine or ritual.

Even as the storm raged outside, the chamber had gone utterly quiet. In that silence, Myr understood something the others would not admit aloud: Bella Lestaire was not useful to them; she had feelings, unnatural feelings that were of no use to him.

CHAPTER THREE

A LIFE OF QUIET MISERY

THE TALK

L ife in the enclaves was a slow erosion of hope. Survival demanded everything: labor, obedience, children. Women were married young; their lives bartered for alliances and the fragile continuation of their people. Magic was taught to them not from choice, but from necessity. When war came, all who could wield a ward or carve a sigil were called to fight.

The lesson had been written in blood. Years ago, a kingdom in the northeast had fallen because its elders forbade women to fight. When vampires descended, the ruling council of men were slaughtered, the women taken and turned. The eastern lands had never been reclaimed.

Among the survivors of that ruin was a young Myr Straus. Clever, ambitious, and unashamed of preserving himself, Myr led those who escaped west across the river. He declared what the old world had refused to accept: men, women, children—*all* must wield Geomancy if humanity were to endure. From this resolve, he built a Sanctum, a school, and a council that would one day command every enclave.

Our Plan For You

Bella Lestaire grew within this order, her beauty and defiance setting her apart as much as her talent. She learned Geomancy as easily as breathing, her instincts sharper than elders twice her age. But to Myr, she was not a prodigy—she was a problem to be managed, a pawn to be placed.

Her fate was decided without her. An alliance had been arranged: Bella would marry Jorric Boyd, grandson of Elder Franc Boyd. It was Loryndor, her father, who delivered the news.

They sat together one evening as the sun bled its last light through the window. Bella had baked bread, and her laughter was bright as she set down a pie. For a fleeting moment, there was warmth between father and daughter. Then Loryndor set his spoon aside.

"Bella," he said softly, "you are no longer a child. The time has come for you to settle with someone who will protect you when I no longer can."

Bella's smile froze. She stared at the dying sun. "So," she said, voice even, "you've decided this without me. All these dinners we've shared, and never once did you mention it."

Loryndor shifted uncomfortably. "I wished to spare you the burden while you were young."

Her eyes snapped to his. "And now?"

"We were thinking," he began, and instantly regretted the slip—

"*We?*" Bella's voice cracked the silence like glass. "Who is this *we* that plans my life, Father?"

He tried to answer with force. "You will do as you are told! This enclave survives only through sacrifice. If you want to remain part of these people, you will fulfill your duty. That is the end of it!"

He rose and left before her fury could rise further. Bella sat in silence, hands clenched in her lap. Her father had faced vampires without fear. But against her, he had fled.

Newlyweds

The wedding was no celebration. There were no flowers, no laughter, no promises whispered in secret. The hall was lit by cold lanternlight, the walls draped in runes that hummed softly, reminders that this union was not born of love but of necessity. Elders recited vows carved from duty, words that tasted like ash on Bella's tongue. She repeated them, her voice steady to all but her own ears, which heard the tremor that slipped in when her gaze strayed toward the door—as if escape were still possible.

Jorric Boyd stood beside her, tall and immovable, his hand resting on hers like a weight rather than a comfort. His eyes never lingered on her face; they fixed instead on the council, on approval, on the sanctity of alliance. When the Heartstone flared to mark the bond, its pale light filled the chamber, but no warmth touched her. Bella felt only the finality of chains closing around her life.

Their first night together was not passion but silence. Jorric extinguished the lanterns without ceremony and lay down with the same mechanical obedience he gave to every task. Bella lay stiff beside him, staring at the ceiling while the wolves howled beyond the walls. She counted cracks in the stone until dawn bled gray light through the shutters, her body present but her soul far away.

From then on, the days blurred into ritual. Jorric woke at dawn, ate bread in silence, and spoke observations about the weather as though such words were intimacy.

"The clouds promise rain tonight," he said one evening. "The drought will end."

Bella forced a smile. "Yes. How thrilling."

Her sarcasm was a small rebellion, one he never noticed. To him, she was duty fulfilled: a wife to bear children, a keeper of hearth and bread. To her, he was stone given flesh, cold and unyielding, incapable of seeing the hollow place where her heart should have lived.

In the marketplace, other women whispered of wedding nights and laughter. Bella only smiled faintly and pressed her hands to her skirts, pretending to share their joy. But inside she knew she had been bartered away, her beauty reduced to coin, her spirit buried beneath the weight of vows forged by men who called it survival.

Her life had become a prison without walls, and Jorric Boyd its dutiful, unfeeling jailer.

The Man of the House

Misery settled into routine, each day a mirror of the last. Jorric Boyd treated his new wife with the same attention he gave to the walls of his house—kept standing, maintained, but never cherished. He spoke of duties and weather, of supply counts and patrol rotations, as if marriage were merely another ledger to balance.

To Bella, silence was the true ruler of their home. She moved through the chambers like a ghost, tending to hearth and bread, all the while sensing that Jorric saw her less as a partner than as a fixture—a piece of furniture in the great order of survival. When her laughter escaped on rare occasions, he glanced at her with puzzlement, as though joy were a language he could not understand.

Then came the night of the hunt. Vampires ambushed the Geomancers returning with a deer. They fought them back, but one was lost—Phineas Drew, keeper of the prison. His absence left a void Elder Myr was quick to exploit.

The elder visited Jorric under the guise of concern. His cane tapped steadily against the stones as he entered, his shadow stretching long across the hearth.

"Your wife," he said, his voice casual, oily, "she bakes bread, does she not?"

Jorric looked up, unsuspecting. "The best."

Myr's lips curled into something that might have been called a smile, if not for the chill it left in the room. "Good. The prison needs a new hand. A baker to feed the captives until judgment is passed. It is a duty she can perform. A wife's happiness, after all, is of no consequence. Her place is to serve her house, her husband, and her people."

Jorric chuckled nervously, then betrayed more than he should. "If I may be honest, Alder—there is no bond between us. If she were to vanish, I would not grieve."

Myr's pale eyes gleamed, sharp as blades catching torchlight. "Then perhaps fortune may one day grant your wish. For now, let her labor in the prison. Such places... accidents happen."

Their laughter was soft, but it carried the weight of a funeral bell. Bella, hidden just beyond the doorway, heard every word. Her blood ran cold. Her husband's indifference had already cut deep, but now it was sharpened by Myr's suggestion—her life weighed not in love or partnership, but in usefulness.

That night, when Jorric returned with forced cheer to tell her the prison "needed her hands," Bella met his words with a bitter smile. She said nothing of what she had overheard, but in her heart, the cracks widened. She was wife, servant, baker, pawn—but never beloved.

And yet, in the thought of leaving Jorric's cold hearth for the grim silence of the prison, Bella felt the first stirring of something dangerous. Hope.

Prison Work

That evening, Jorric returned home with a cheer too forced to be genuine. He set his boots down by the door, as if the simple act of stomping off mud could mask the weight of the words he carried.

"Bella," he said, his tone almost rehearsed, "I have news. The prison needs you. It will be good for you—something to fill your days."

Bella looked up from the table, her hands still dusted with flour. Her eyebrow arched. "And when did you decide I would take such work?"

"It is an opportunity. A choice," Jorric said stiffly, though the word "choice" sounded brittle in his mouth, as though even he did not believe it.

Her lips curved into a bitter smile. "A slave wife, with choices. How generous."

He ignored the barb, settling into his chair as though the matter were finished. For him, it was. For her, it was another chain, another duty pressed upon her without voice or consent.

Yet as she sat there, listening to the crackle of the fire and the hollow scrape of his spoon against the bowl, something unexpected flickered within her. The thought of being away from this cold hearth—away from the man who called himself her husband—was a relief so sharp it nearly made her tremble.

She wanted to argue further, to spit defiance into the silence, but exhaustion weighed her tongue. What difference would it make? In this house, her words were stones thrown against a fortress wall.

At last, she nodded. "Very well."

And so began Bella's new existence—not wife, not daughter, but baker of bread for prisoners awaiting judgment. The irony was not lost on her. Her marriage was a prison, her life a sentence without end. And yet within those damp walls, behind iron bars and wards that hummed like caged storms, there lay something her own hearth could not offer: escape.

It was no true freedom, not yet. But in her hollow days, it was something. And for Bella Lestaire, whose spirit still smoldered beneath the ash of obedience, even the smallest taste of freedom could spark a fire.

CHAPTER FOUR

A PRISON TO ESCAPE

ORIN AND THE PACK

B ella did everything with quiet precision. Faithful to her husband, obedient to her father's memory, she carried her burdens without faltering. Even in misery, she could not bring herself to cut corners; bread was baked to perfection, her household kept in order. It was what her father expected, and though she raged against him in private, she never dishonored his lessons.

Yet her only escape lay behind iron bars.

The prison was a bleak place of damp stone and stale air, where the hum of Geomancer wards pressed like a constant weight against the skull. It was a thankless duty: feeding outcasts, traitors, and captured monsters from other factions. Bella moved in ritual—porridge ladled, bread placed, bowls passed through bars. One cell after another, like clockwork.

And then she found him.

Orin.

He bore the werewolf curse, but something in him was... incomplete. Even under full moons he did not change. His body carried scars, his wrists bore chains, yet his eyes were clear—haunted, but human. Unlike the feral beasts she had glimpsed, Orin was quiet, restrained. The elders kept him alive, curious about his difference, and Bella, against all reason, was drawn to him.

One evening, as she turned to leave, a guard's boots struck sharply on the stones, startling her. She flinched. From the shadows, Orin's hand slipped through the bars. His calloused fingers brushed hers—only for an instant. Yet the touch was enough. A spark, terrifying and impossible, passed between them. A promise. A plea.

Feeding the Wolf

The bread was stale, but to Orin it tasted like freedom. He ate with the hunger of a wolf who hadn't seen a hunt in weeks, tearing at the crust while still trying to keep his dignity intact. Bella watched him, her own pulse racing. This was reckless, dangerous. She should never have come here. And yet... seeing the way his eyes softened in gratitude, she couldn't regret it.

For one brief moment, she saw the man beneath the chains—the gentleness, the quiet strength, the Orin who refused to let the Geomancers break him. It was enough to make her chest ache.

She pressed the empty cloth into her sleeve, ready to slip back to her quarters. "Don't thank me," she whispered. "You'll make me foolish enough to come again."

Orin's lips curved in the faintest shadow of a smile. "Then I will thank you twice."

Her heart stumbled at the words. She left quickly, forcing her steps to stay quiet on the cold stone floors. By the time she reached her chamber, her hands still trembled. She told herself it had been only a kindness, nothing more. But in the Sanctum, nothing remained secret for long.

The next morning, the apprentices whispered.

Bella kept her face a mask of calm as she walked the training yard, her eyes sweeping over the line of students shaping stones into precise lattices. Their hands worked, but their voices betrayed them.

"...she brings him food..."

"...talks to him in the dark..."

"...the prisoner smiles when she comes..."

Bella's stomach turned to ice. The words were fragments, carried on the wind, but they were enough. They weren't talking about any prisoner. They were talking about Orin.

At the edge of the yard, Jorric stood watching. His lips did not move, but his eyes gleamed with cruel satisfaction, as though he enjoyed watching her squirm under the whispers. When one apprentice faltered, letting his lattice collapse in a spray of gravel, Jorric snapped his fingers. A stone whip lashed across the boy's back, leaving a shallow welt.

The lesson was clear: mistakes meant punishment. But Bella saw something else. Jorric had done it for her benefit, his gaze cutting to hers like a blade. The cruelty wasn't only for the boy—it was a reminder. *He knew.*

She forced her voice steady as she addressed the apprentices. "Focus. If your minds wander, your work fails. And failure here is death."

The whispers quieted, but the seed had been planted. Rumors were growing, roots spreading through stone. Bella walked on, her face cold, her heart burning. She had given Orin a piece of light in the dark—and now, the darkness threatened to swallow them both.

A Whisper Through Stone

The corridors of the Sanctum were hushed that night, the kind of silence that carried every sound like a blade through flesh. Bella lingered in the shadows outside the training yard, her hands full of scrolls she had been ordered to deliver. She should have gone straight to the archives. Instead, she froze.

Two apprentices leaned against the iron gates, voices low but urgent.

"Did you see him today?" one whispered. "After the lashings? He stood like it was nothing."

The other scoffed, but there was unease in the sound. "That wolf's pride is poison. The Elders should've broken him by now."

Bella's heart hammered. They were speaking of Orin.

"He didn't beg," the first muttered. "Didn't even curse them. Just... stared. Like he pitied us. Like we were the ones bound."

A pause. Then a softer, almost fearful confession: "When they set the younger ones to throw stones at him, I... I couldn't."

"You'll get yourself lashed for that kind of talk," the other snapped. "Forget him. He's nothing but an example."

Their footsteps retreated down the hall, leaving Bella in the quiet crackle of torchlight. But their words had settled into her bones.

Later, she passed the training yard herself. Moonlight silvered the ground, falling on the lone figure chained in its center. Orin knelt, back straight despite the iron biting into his wrists. His body bore fresh marks, but his gaze was steady, turned skyward as though he were listening to something beyond the walls.

He looked nothing like a broken man.

Bella pressed her hand to the cold stone of the archway, a strange ache blooming in her chest. She had seen prisoners curse, weep, collapse into themselves. But Orin bore his suffering with a dignity that unsettled her. The apprentices saw it. She saw it.

For the first time in years, she found herself wishing for someone else's strength. Not for survival, not for vengeance—simply to remember what it felt like to be whole.

When his eyes shifted toward her, catching the faintest flicker of her torchlight, she pulled back into the dark. But the image lingered: a man punished for defiance, yet unbroken.

A whisper of a thought surfaced, dangerous and undeniable. *If he can endure this, then maybe... so can I.*

CHAPTER FIVE

LESSONS IN THE YARD

DIGNITY

The clang of iron doors echoed through the Sanctum's eastern yard, a sound that made the apprentices stand straighter and quiet their nervous chatter. The prison yard was rarely opened for lessons, and when it was, the day promised a spectacle.

The Magisters led them in rows, their black robes whispering against stone. At the center of the yard stood Orin. Shackled at wrists and ankles, the chains rattled as he shifted his weight, but his back was straight, his shoulders squared. Dirt streaked his skin where he had been forced to his knees, yet there was no bow in him. He was a wolf, caged, but unbroken.

"Behold," Magister Jorric said, his voice sharp enough to carry to every corner of the yard. "The cost of defiance. This beast raided our borders, tore through our wards, and believed his savagery could match our order. What is he now? A tool for your learning. Nothing more."

He paced around Orin like a jackal circling prey. The apprentices watched, wide-eyed. Some curious. Some frightened. Some—too young to know better—smirking.

"You will learn today that strength without discipline is nothing. You will see that even a wolf, with all his fangs and fury, can be brought low. This is the way of the world: magic rules, and beasts kneel."

Jorric's hand flicked, and the chains binding Orin tightened, forcing him down into the dirt. A ripple of laughter broke from a few of the bolder apprentices. Orin's jaw tightened, but his eyes remained steady, fixed on some point beyond the wall. He did not give Jorric the satisfaction of a cry.

"Strike him," Jorric ordered suddenly.

The apprentices stiffened. A boy stepped forward, hesitant, clutching a practice staff. He looked back at the others, then raised it high. The wood came down across Orin's shoulder with a dull crack. Orin did not flinch. The boy struck again, harder this time.

This time, Orin's lips moved. His voice was low, ragged, almost lost under the scrape of chains:

"Love is not weakness," he rasped. "It is endurance."

The words hung in the yard like a forbidden spell. The boy froze mid-swing. Even Bella felt them lodge in her chest, sharp as a blade.

Jorric's eyes narrowed. "Harder!" he barked.

The boy lifted the staff once more, but his arms shook. It was not Orin's strength that unnerved him, but the calm in his eyes, the truth of his words. The wolf did not look at his chains. He looked at them—apprentices, children of the Sanctum—and something in that gaze made the boy lower his weapon.

Coward, Jorric's glare said. He shoved the boy aside and called another forward. And another. But each strike landed on a body that refused to bend, and each young face wavered under the weight of Orin's defiance. The phrase repeated itself, unspoken but echoing: *Love is not weakness. It is endurance.*

By the time Jorric dismissed them, the apprentices' eyes no longer sparkled with curiosity. They carried something heavier now—a question unspoken: If a beast can endure this, what does that make us?

Orin was dragged away, chains clattering, his steps still steady. Bella could not look away. In the space of a lesson meant to humiliate, she had seen a truth the Magisters could not hide: strength was not in cruelty or in chains. Strength was in restraint, in endurance, in the quiet refusal to break.

And that night, when she returned to the cells with bread in her hands, she no longer told herself it was pity that guided her. It was something else. Something dangerous.

Weakness or Endurance?

The cell was small, little more than a hollow carved into the Sanctum's foundations, its walls slick with condensation and the stink of old stone. Runes burned faintly on the iron door, their glow a reminder that even the air inside was shackled.

Bella lingered outside longer than she should have. She had seen him earlier in the yard—Orin, bound, tortured, yet unbroken. His words had unsettled her, lodged in her chest like a shard of glass. *Love is not weakness. It is endurance.*

It should have repelled her. Instead, it drew her here.

The guards were gone. Only silence remained. She pressed her palm to the runes, feeling the faint thrum of power, then whispered the counter-syllables she had memorized from watching Magistra Lycah too many times. The sigils sputtered, dimmed, then fell quiet.

The door groaned open.

Inside, Orin sat cross-legged on the floor, his chains pooled around him. His skin was burned raw where the runes had seared him, but his posture was upright, his expression calm. When he lifted his eyes to hers, there was no bitterness. Only recognition.

"You shouldn't be here," he said softly, his voice ragged but steady.

"Neither should you," Bella answered before she could stop herself.

A flicker of a smile ghosted across his lips. "That's true enough."

She stepped inside, though every part of her screamed to turn back. The walls pressed close, the air thick, but she forced herself to meet his gaze. She thought of the apprentices in the yard, their frightened faces, their hope snuffed out by Lycah's cruelty. And she thought of him, speaking words that had been forbidden, holding himself against pain that would have broken any of them.

"Why did you say it?" she asked, her voice low. "Why tell them love is strength, when you knew they would punish you for it?"

His answer was simple. "Because it's true. And sometimes the truth is worth bleeding for."

Her breath caught. For a moment, the chains and the stone and the silence fell away, and she saw not a prisoner but a man—one who refused to surrender what little light he had left.

She sank onto the cold floor opposite him. "They'll kill you for it."

"Maybe." He tilted his head, studying her. "But maybe someone will remember. Maybe you will."

The words struck her harder than any blow. She wanted to deny them; to remind him she was a Geomancer bound to the Sanctum, but the truth was already carved into her bones. She would remember. She already had.

Outside, the stone walls groaned under the weight of the Sanctum. But in the cage of stone, a fragile, impossible seed had been planted.

CHAPTER SIX
THE WOLVES

WILD BERRY BREAD AND DREAMS

Bella risked more than she dared admit when she baked the bread. She had steeped water with wild berries for weeks, a secret indulgence. Orin had once confessed, in a rare unguarded moment, that the taste reminded him of boyhood—of racing through southern forests with his brother, of a time before the curse had become a cage. Bella carried the loaf like contraband as she descended into the prison.

But when she arrived, her heart froze.

"Where is the wolf prisoner?" she demanded.

The guards exchanged smirks. "Activities," one chuckled darkly. "Don't worry, lady. He'll be brought back."

Hours later, chains clattered, and doors banged open. Orin was dragged across the stones, unconscious, his knees scraping, his chest torn and bleeding. They chained him again and left, laughing as though cruelty were sport.

Bella forced her face into a mask of indifference until the guards departed. Then she rushed to the bars, her hands trembling. With her Geomancy she could have closed his wounds in a breath, but suspicion would fall on her at once. So, she did what she could—pressed cloth to stop the bleeding, whispered apologies as tears pricked her eyes.

"I am sorry, Orin. I wanted to bring you something sweet. Instead..." Her voice broke. She pushed the berry bread through the bars. "Rest. I will come again soon."

His hand caught hers weakly. "Stay." His voice was ragged, but the plea was clear.

She sank to the floor outside his cell.

"Tell me of your family," Bella said gently, refusing his attempts to steer the talk toward her father and husband. "I want to know them. Your brother. Your father."

Orin smiled faintly through the pain. "My brother, Bryn, is swifter than I. Reckless, daring. We challenged each other from the time we could walk. He is the storm; I... the stone." He paused, his eyes shadowed. "He left, before I was taken. Sought power beyond the pack. I told him: 'A lone wolf is a dead wolf.' But he went anyway."

Bella leaned closer. "And your father?"

Orin took the bread in his scarred hands and bit into it. His eyes widened. "Wild berries."

"Yes," she said, smiling softly. "I remembered."

He closed his eyes, savoring it, as though the taste had carried him home. "Emor, our father, was Alpha once. Wise, strong, merciless when needed. He taught us loyalty; taught us the pack is life. Even now, old as he is, he remains a strategist, the mind behind every strike. His words still guide me: *A lone wolf is a dead wolf.*"

Bella tilted her head. "And your mother?"

His gaze fell. "I never knew her. Father said she died when Bryn and I were pups. He would not speak of her." He forced another bite of bread, and the sweetness seemed to soften the weight of his grief.

Bella touched the bars, her fingers brushing his. "Do not frighten me again. Next time, wait for me before you are beaten."

Despite the pain, Orin laughed, low and rough. "I will."

From One Elder's Eyes to Another's Ears

Bella lingered longer than she should have, her hand still warm from Orin's fleeting touch. She wrapped her cloak tighter and moved toward the exit.

The corridor was darker than usual, the wards humming faintly against the cold. A cane tapped the stones ahead, and her breath caught. Elder Myk Yonder stepped into view, tall and severe, his silver hair tied back, his eyes pale as glass. He was known less for speeches than for silence, the kind that made men uneasy.

"Late, Bella," he said softly, his voice echoing down the corridor. "The prison is no place for wandering hearts."

Her chest tightened, but she forced a calm smile. "I was ensuring the last bowls were delivered. Nothing more."

Myk's gaze flicked past her, toward Orin's cell. The werewolf did not move, but even in stillness his presence was undeniable. Myk lingered a moment, studying the air between them, as though weighing an invisible thread. Then he nodded once.

"See that it remains so," he said. "Affection is weakness. You know what becomes of weakness in this world."

His cane tapped once, sharp against the stone, before he disappeared into the shadows. Bella stood frozen, her pulse hammering in her throat. She knew now that her secret had been seen.

What she could not know was that Elder Myk would carry word to Elder Myr Straus before dawn. And between them, in whispers and schemes, Bella's fate was already being woven into the cold designs of the council.

A Night of Dreams

That night, Orin dreamt.

He was young again, racing with Bryn through the woods, laughter ringing as they dashed toward a berry tree. Bryn always won, always faster, always daring. Then the dream shifted.

Bryn stood beneath the full moon. *"Tonight is my last with you, brother. I travel west. The moon will guide me."* Orin begged him to stay, pleaded that their father needed them both. But Bryn only turned, and smoke swallowed him.

The dream twisted again. Orin ran with the pack, hunting. But the prey was Bella. Terrek Greybeard, cruel even among wolves, toyed with her, snapping at her heels before lunging for her throat. Orin screamed, but the scene warped further. A boy wept beside his father's corpse, and Terrek's jaws gaped for the child's face. Orin hurled himself between them, standing firm, refusing the bloodlust. His kindness—his fatal flaw—held the beast at bay.

Orin woke gasping, his chest heaving. The torchlight of the prison burned away the visions, but the truth remained: it was his refusal to kill that had led to his capture. Protecting a human during a skirmish, defying his own pack, he had been ensnared by a wolf-pelt lasso. His last sight before darkness had been four Geomancers staring down at him, deciding he was too strange to kill outright.

He was not outcast. Not free. Not wolf. Not man. Only prisoner. And yet, for the first time, he was not entirely alone.

Dangerous Game

As dangerous a game that both Bella and Orin were playing, the visits became frequent and longer. In secret, their bond deepened. Bella lingered by his cell long after her duties were done. Sometimes, her hand would linger against his through the bars. Once, she caught herself smiling as she walked home; Jorric, mistaking it for joy in marriage, never guessed she was carrying Orin's words in her heart.

Orin's world both horrified and fascinated her. He spoke of the pack, where weakness was hunted, and the moon was God and torment alike. Of the ritual transformations that stripped away humanity until only hunger remained.

"It is madness," he admitted. "A sacred madness. Those who cannot embrace it are cast out. Or killed."

Bella shivered. "And yet... here you are. Gentle, kind. Why?"

Orin's eyes, glinting in the dim torchlight, softened. "Because savagery is easy. Kindness... is the hardest fight of all."

Listening to Orin speak was difficult for Bella to imagine that all of his kin were brutes and beasts. One evening, when their words had worn thin, but their silence had grown full, Bella whispered the thought that had been gnawing at her.

"If I helped you escape... if I left this place, went west of the river with you—would your people accept me?"

Orin's face tightened. "No. To them, the scent of a Geomancer is poison. They would never accept you. You are their enemy. And yet..." He reached for her hand, barely touching her fingertips. "If the world were different, Bella, I would take you there myself."

The words cut her. She turned away, hiding the ache in her chest. "Then I must go. Goodbye, Orin."

"Goodbye, Bella."

CHAPTER SEVEN

A NIGHT OF PASSION

THE PRISONER AND HIS VISITOR

The full moon burned silver in the heavens, a sovereign eye watching all. The Geomancers had ridden out to clash with the vampire host near the river, their patrols gone, their watchful eyes turned elsewhere. Bella stood in the shadows of her home, her husband's absence a hollow echo, her heart hammering with a truth she could no longer bury.

Tonight, she would see Orin.

The air was damp with fog and pine, cloaking her steps in secrecy as she slipped to the prison. Inside, the halls were chaos—bread left half-eaten, candles guttering on the stone floor, keys carelessly abandoned. She gathered them with trembling hands. This night, the walls of order and obedience would break.

When she opened the cell, Orin's eyes met hers. At first, he was the scarred prisoner, the chained beast. But when recognition sparked, he was only a man—her man—his eyes softened by the light of the moon.

"Bella," he rasped, voice heavy with disbelief and fear. "If they catch you—"

She pressed a finger to his lips. "Let them. I came to live. To feel. To be with you."

And then she was in his arms.

The First Night

Their lips met with hesitance, then urgency. His hands, rough from battle and chains, trembled as if he feared she might vanish. Her kiss was fire and freedom, a rebellion against duty and despair. The prison fell away. The world fell away. There was only them.

He held her as though she were something sacred, fragile, and yet she felt his strength in every motion, every caress. The passion that followed was not just flesh against flesh, but soul against soul—two prisoners breaking free together, if only for a night.

When dawn bled across the horizon, she left him with tears on her lips and his name pressed against her heart.

The Meetings After

It did not end that night. The moon pulled her back again and again, her footsteps growing bolder, her heart ever more entangled.

She would bring him bread laced with herbs and wild berries, water scented with mint, and her stories—of childhood, of rebellion, of the suffocating silence of her marriage. In return, he gave her tales of the wild, of the pack's brutal laws, of his brother Bryn and his father Emor, and of the constant battle with the beast inside him.

"Your world is order," Orin once said, pressing his forehead to hers. "Mine is chaos. But in you, Bella, I see a third world. A place where both can exist."

Sometimes they spoke until the stars paled. Sometimes they touched—her hand through the bars, his fingers trembling as though that single connection meant more than life. And sometimes, when courage overcame caution, she stole inside his cell again, where kisses deepened into a passion fierce enough to burn away the iron chains of reality.

Shadows of Suspicion

But shadows gathered.

The guards spoke of strange sounds in the night. Elder Myr's sharp gaze lingered on Bella when she passed, his eyes narrowing as though he could smell secrets in the air. Even Jorric, blind as he was to her sorrow, began to notice her smiles that did not belong to him.

And yet, Bella could not stop. Each meeting was a flame, and she was the moth. She told herself she could still control it, still keep the truth hidden. But in her heart, she knew: the world was watching. The moon was watching. And soon, someone else would too.

CHAPTER EIGHT

A TREACHEROUS SECRET

BEAST WITHIN

A month passed since the night of the full moon, and a subtle but undeniable change crept into Bella's body. At first it was only faint nausea, a quickening of breath, a new sharpness in her senses. But as dawn broke one morning, she found herself hunched in the field, retching the bread she had eaten earlier, her hands trembling as though the earth itself rejected her.

Jorric came upon her, his shadow long in the morning light. "Bella," he said, brows furrowed. "You've looked unwell for weeks. What's happening?"

"I am fine," she replied too quickly, brushing the sweat from her brow. "The meal last night... it didn't sit well."

But in her heart, she knew the truth.

The morning sickness. The cravings. The strange surges of strength beneath her skin. She was with child.

And she could not know whose.

A cold dread pierced her like the blade of a dagger. If it was Jorric's, the child would be a human—perhaps even a Geomancer of promise. But if it was Orin's... if the forbidden passion she had surrendered to beneath the full moon bore fruit... then what grew within her was no simple life. It was something else. Something the world had never seen.

A War Within Herself

Her mind became a battlefield.

What have I done? she asked herself in the quiet of her chamber. *I have betrayed my husband. Betrayed my father. Betrayed my people. And yet... was it betrayal to seize a single night of love in a lifetime of misery?*

The guilt gnawed at her, but so did the memory of Orin's arms, his voice, the passion that had awakened a part of her soul she had never known. Jorric had never touched her heart. Orin had claimed it with a glance.

When Jorric returned the day after his battle, exhausted but proud, Bella had already hidden every trace of what had transpired. She offered him bread, her voice steady, though her mind was still in Orin's cell.

"Well," Jorric said between bites, "it takes more than vampires to rid the world of me."

Bella only smiled faintly. Her body was here, but her heart was elsewhere.

Concealment

Determined to protect her secret, Bella turned to sympathetic magic. She wove a veil of concealment around her body, a charm that masked the early signs of her condition from casual eyes. Loose-fitting tunics hid the swell of her belly; charms of misdirection shielded her aura from those who might probe too deeply. She moved with care, her every gesture calculated to silence suspicion.

But the moon betrayed her.

On the next full moon, pain tore through her body like molten iron. She clutched her abdomen, writhing in silence, her sweat falling in cold beads. The child within her responded—not like a human babe, but as though it were bound to the lunar tide. On the following cycle, the pain grew worse. The truth settled on her heart like a stone: *This is no child of Jorric's. This is Orin's.*

A mixed blood. A cursed union. A secret that could shatter her world.

The Husband's Pride

Her secret endured for a time, but her body could only hold it for so long.

One morning, Jorric found her doubled over in the garden. He mistook her silence for coyness, her nausea for a miracle. "Bella!" he exclaimed, puffing his chest with pride. "Were you keeping this as a surprise for me?"

Her blood ran cold.

"You... you know?" she stammered, terrified of what his eyes might truly see.

"Of course," Jorric said, smugness curling his lips. "I've been watching. You've not been yourself. Now I understand. This child will seal the alliance. The council will rejoice."

Bella forced a smile, though shame and fear churned in her chest. In his arrogance, Jorric never doubted the child was his. He saw it as a victory, proof of his manhood, a gift to the enclave.

And Bella—cold, terrified, and cunning—let him believe the lie.

The Treachery of Silence

For the first time in her life, Bella played the dutiful wife without protest. She nodded at Jorric's boasts, accepted his empty pride, and hid her trembling hands in her skirts. But within her, two truths warred like beasts in a cage:

She carried a child of impossible blood.

And she carried a secret that could unmake everything.

Each night, when the moonlight touched her window, she whispered to the life within her, not knowing whether it was blessing or curse:

You are mine. And whatever the world says, I will not let them take you.

But even as she whispered, shadows seemed to gather at the corners of her home. Elder Myr's eyes lingered on her longer. Elder Myk Yonder asked strange, careful questions. The prison guards muttered of strange happenings in the night.

The treacherous secret within her was no longer hers alone.

The Last Sanctuary

The prison had become Bella's true home. Not the cold stone dwelling she shared with Jorric, not the silent halls of the Sanctum, but the dim-lit cell where Orin lay chained. Here, within walls meant for despair, she found life.

She slipped in under the veil of night, the keys hidden in her cloak, her every step careful, deliberate. The moon was only a crescent now, but its pale light spilled through the narrow window and cast Orin in silver. His eyes opened at her presence, and for the first time in weeks, his expression softened into something like peace.

"You came," he whispered, as though her arrival was not certain, but a miracle renewed each time.

"I will always come," Bella answered, though her voice trembled. In her belly, the secret stirred, pressing against her lie, reminding her of the peril they both faced.

Conversations of Truth

They sat close, separated by iron, their hands brushing through the bars. Their conversations were no longer of survival alone, but of dreams, whispered like prayers.

"I dream of the forest," Orin said, his eyes distant. "Of running free with Bryn, of the rivers that smell of pine and stone. I dream of a world where my hands are not chained, where my heart is not caged."

"And I," Bella replied, "dream of a life where love is not called treason. Where the only law is the bond between two souls."

"You speak of a world that does not exist."

"Then we must make it," she said fiercely, her hand tightening on his.

Orin smiled then, not the smile of a prisoner, but the smile of a man who believed, even for a moment, that freedom was possible.

The Fragile Flame

When she dared, she slipped inside his cell again, where their stolen embraces blurred the line between defiance and destiny. The prison's walls seemed to fade when she lay against him, her head on his chest, his heartbeat a song of strength and sorrow.

"Bella," he said one night, his voice low, almost breaking, "if you are ever in danger, you must flee. Do not think of me—think of yourself."

But Bella shook her head, her eyes flashing like the embers of a dying fire. "No. My fate is bound to yours, Orin. If they condemn you, they condemn me. And if they kill me, they kill what lives inside me."

Orin stilled, his eyes wide, as though her words had revealed more than she intended. But Bella pressed her lips to his, silencing any question, burying the truth in the heat of their kiss.

The Encroaching Storm

Each meeting was more dangerous than the last. Guards had begun to notice the way she lingered. Elder Myr's questions had grown sharper, probing. Elder Myk Yonder watched her like a hawk, his silence more menacing than words.

And yet, she returned. Again and again, drawn by love, by desperation, by the knowledge that soon, the choice would be stolen from her.

On their final night together, as dawn threatened, Orin held her face in his hands, his eyes fierce. "Bella, if you vanish one day and I never see you again, know this—I loved you more than the moon, more than the pack, more than freedom itself."

Tears burned her eyes. "And I, you. Whatever comes, Orin, whatever curse or blessing this love has brought—we were alive. Truly alive."

The iron door closed behind her with a heavy echo, and Bella knew with chilling certainty: the walls of secrecy were closing in.

CHAPTER NINE
BETRAYAL

WHO IS HE?

Jorric's satisfaction was a fragile thing, a thin shell over a storm. He was a man of logic and order, yet something gnawed at him. Bella's obedience was too perfect, her smiles too precise, her gaze too often distant.

It was Elder Myk Yonder who first leaned close one evening at the Sanctum.

"You watch her carefully, Jorric. The prison is a dangerous place, filled with temptations of a darker sort."

The words seemed harmless, but they lodged deep in Jorric's mind. Days later, Elder Myr Straus confirmed the seed Myk had planted.

"Your wife is diligent," Myr had said, his voice measured, "but diligence can be a mask. One must be certain her loyalty is not... compromised."

The hints became a steady drip, each whisper eroding the trust Jorric clung to. Soon, suspicion was no longer a passing thought, but a truth waiting to be proven.

Shadows in the Prison

He went to the prison, driven by the elders' carefully sown doubts.

"Hello, Randall."

The guard straightened, fumbling with his keys. "Ah, Sir Jorric. To what do I owe the pleasure?"

"I have a question. When my wife visits... have you noticed anything strange? Does she linger with anyone?"

Randall shook his head earnestly. "No, sir. Lady Bella is always kind. She brings me bread—always warm, always fresh. A blessing."

Bread. Always bread.

Jorric's lip curled, though he hid it. He pressed deeper into the corridors, and at Orin's cell he found it: a basket lined with crimson cloth, a token too personal to be chance. His heart went cold.

The Elders' Hand in the Snare

When he returned to the Sanctum, Myr was waiting, as though he had known.

"You found something, didn't you?" the old man murmured, his voice oily with satisfaction. "Trust your instincts, Jorric. She dishonors you—and more importantly, endangers us all."

It was no longer suspicion. It was certainty, sharpened by the elders' whispers.

The final stroke came from a captured pup, dosed with truth-serum. The creature's slurred words sealed Bella's fate:

"A human woman... she comes to the kind wolf... she stayed the night of the full moon..."

Myr and Myk did not need to say more. Jorric's fury crystallized.

The Spell of Truth

That night, Jorric wove his spell at the Heartstone, crimson light binding truth to betrayal. When the glow clung to Bella, he knew.

"You have broken the sacred bond," he whispered. "You have endangered us all."

The door opened. Two Geomancers stepped inside, already summoned, already waiting.

"Take her away," Jorric said, his voice like iron. "She has much to explain to the elders."

Myr Straus watched from the shadows, a faint smile curling his lips. The trap was complete.

Iron closed around her wrists. She was dragged from her home, the child within her twisting in defiance.

They cast her into Orin's old cell—the place where love had blossomed now turned to a tomb of betrayal. The irony burned her heart, but worse was the knowledge of what the elders planned: her child taken, studied, treated as a specimen rather than a soul.

Alone in the dark, Bella pressed trembling hands to her belly.

They will not take you. Not while I still breathe.

COUNCIL OF SHADOWS

Myr's Ambition

The Sanctum's chamber was lit only by the cold glow of the Heartstone, its surface pulsing with a crimson hue that made the carved walls bleed with shadow. The air was heavy with incense, the bitter smoke coiling like serpents around the assembled elders.

Elder Myr Straus stood at the center, his hunch and wrinkled face casting monstrous silhouettes on the stone. Beside him was Elder Myk Yonder, his frame tall and rigid, his voice the sharp edge of iron. Between them, Bella knelt in chains, her hair spilling forward, her face pale but defiant.

Myr's voice cut the silence.

"Brothers and sisters of the enclave, we gather tonight not for the trivial matters of crops or wards, but for survival itself. For betrayal has crept into our midst, clothed in innocence, hidden in beauty."

A murmur rippled through the chamber.

Myk stepped forward, his words precise and merciless.

"Bella Lestaire has consorted with the enemy. With a beast. Not only has she broken her sacred vows, but she carries within her a life not wholly human. A corruption. A hybrid. A threat to all we guard."

The words struck like stones. Some elders recoiled in shock, others leaned forward, eyes glinting with fear.

Myr raised his hand, commanding silence.

"Do not think of this as a child. No. It is a weapon. One forged not by our hands but by fate's cruelty. If it lives, it could be the end of us... or the very tool we need to crush our enemies."

The council erupted—voices clashing, fear against ambition.

"It must be destroyed!" cried Elder Veyla, her voice shrill. "Even now its blood taints her body. Do you not feel the pull of the moon upon it?"

"No," countered Elder Thalos, younger and bold. "If such a creature lives, it could become our strongest ward against werewolves and vampires alike. We would wield what they fear most."

Myr's eyes glinted with satisfaction. This was what he wanted: division, desperation, the chance to position himself as the only one with the wisdom to decide.

He turned slowly to Bella.

"Speak, child. Tell us the truth of your heart. Tell us what this life inside you truly is."

Bella lifted her chin. Her chains rattled, but her voice did not waver.

"This life is mine. It is not yours to dissect or destroy. It is not a weapon. It is not a monster. It is a child—and I will die before I let you touch it."

The chamber fell silent, her words like a spark in a hall of dry timber.

Myr let the silence stretch, then smiled his prune-faced smile. "You see, my fellow elders? Even in chains, she defies us. Such fire can only come from the wolf she lies with. Her words condemn her as surely as any proof."

Myk's voice followed like a hammer blow. "The question is not whether she is guilty. She is. The question is whether we kill the child... or raise it as ours."

The Heartstone pulsed, red as fresh blood, casting the council in light and shadow. The decision hung in the air like a sword above Bella's neck.

CHAPTER ELEVEN

THE TRIAL

LESSON LEARNED

T he trial was not held in a marble hall or behind carved doors. It was held in the open heart of the settlement, where every face could be witness and every voice could bear judgment. The council of elders sat elevated on a low arc of stone, the Heartstone's cold glow painting their faces in a relentless light. Below them, the villagers clustered women with hands folded, men with jaws clenched, children pressed to their mothers' skirts. The world had come to watch a woman be unmade.

Bella was cast before them on her knees, wrists bound, her belly a visible traitor between the ropes. Her hair fell in a dark curtain, her face pale but not cowed. Jorric stood at the council's side—no longer her husband in tenderness, but the accuser in duty. His face had lost its softness. A satisfaction that had once been fragile had grown hard as iron.

The spectacle was for Myr more than for Jorric. Myr had fed suspicion to Jorric like a slow poison, whispered it at twilight and dawn, guided him until the man's doubts turned to a blade. As the crowd murmured, Myr drew Jorric aside beneath the shadow of the elders' seats.

"Remember what is at stake," Myr said quietly, words slick with purpose. "Our order does not survive sentiment. Convince Loryndor if you must. Make him yield, and all will go as needed."

Jorric nodded, his features set. The old man's whisper had hardened him into an instrument.

Myr needed Loryndor. The younger father had been summoned with a formal parchment—an urgent call that left no space for refusal. Jasper, a pale-faced student and errand-runner, had rushed the message to the Lestaire cottage that morning. The letter's tone was precise as the blade: attendance required. Failure to appear would be taken as a forfeiture of any say in his daughter's fate.

When Loryndor arrived he saw what every other face in the square had seen for hours: Bella chained before the elders, exposed to the judgment of their people. Rage and despair warred across his features. He tried to rush forward; Myr met him like a rock.

"Calm yourself," Myr intoned, an actor of sorrow. "This was not my wish. But the evidence is grave. She has betrayed the coven—consorted with a prisoner, brought a corrupted thing into her womb. You must understand, Loryndor. The Heartstone does not lie."

Loryndor faltered. The name of the Heartstone had weight; Myr used it like a gavel. He could not bear to learn the truth there, at the altar; he steadied himself on the counsel's words instead. He begged—softly, a father's plea, to spare her life. Myr's answer was measured: mercy in form, punishment in practice. "We will not take her life while you breathe, friend," he said, "but she must be taught the cost of such treason."

The crowd's murmurs swelled into cries. Jorric stepped forward and spoke with cold clarity, shaping the outrage into a law-bound argument.

"She has tainted our bloodline," he told them, voice ringing. "She has endangered the survival of every child in our coven. Traditions are not sentimentalities; they are shields. She has pierced ours."

Magistra Lycah, pale and severe, rose and added the final piece. "The Heartstone has confirmed it. The life within her answers to the moon. It is not wholly human. We will not make the mistake of mercy when survival is at stake."

The verdict hung in the square like an oath.

Then Myr signaled. From a rear cart the guards brought Orin forward—bound, raw from the moon's travail, barely more than a shadow of the man Bella had known. The crowd sucked the air in; their hunger for spectacle was a thing the elders fed. Orin's eyes found Bella's; there was no softness left, only the bruised recognition of two lives twisted together by fate.

They did not speak of slow, surgical cruelty. They did not need to. The Elders chose spectacle over discretion: punishment that would teach, humiliation to mark a lesson, pain that would be witnessed and remembered. Myr's voice took on a cadence of pedagogue and prosecutor.

"Let our people see," he intoned. "Let them understand what happens when one of us fraternizes with the beasts that would devour us. Let there be no doubt left in any mind."

The guards had their instruments—tools designed to break pride, to silence voice and sight, to make a lesson out of living flesh. Bella's breath hitched as the first sounds of Orin's punishment began in the chill air. She rose to her feet, eyes blazing, and the hooded constable behind her fastened a strap to hold her head steady so she would not look away.

"Stop!" she cried. Her voice rose above the hum of the crowd, a sudden bird call. "This is not justice!"

Jorric's hand stayed steady; he did not waver. "Order demands it," he said, and in his expression, there was no triumph, only a hard resignation—a man made cruel by counsel and conviction.

Orin's thrashings slowed, then ceased. When at last the guards dragged him to his feet, his shoulders sagged; whatever sound he had made was gone—not wordless through mercy but muted by the cruelty of those who would teach lesson with pain. He collapsed and was left in the dust, his strength bled away by punishment and the cold, clinical Geomancy that had been turned on him for the crowd's assurance.

Bella's whole body trembled. She screamed again, a raw, broken sound that rose and broke against the stone. Loryndor's face, which had reddened with fury, now crumpled with a grief that would not be undone. He looked at his daughter and looked away; there was nothing left in him but the hollow of a man who had been robbed of his child's innocence.

Myr's eyes shone in the Heartstone's light. He turned to the circle of elders and the watching village and declared, as if bestowing a benediction:

"You see now what happens to those who treat our covenant lightly. Let them carry this memory in their bones—let the next generation know and fear it." He paused, and his voice dropped, a private rasp the crowd could not hear. "Take both of them away. Let him be left to expire beneath our warding. Let her bear witness to the end of what she created. In time, we will decide what to do with the child."

They dragged Orin away. They led Bella back to the same cell where she had first found him—where she had first knelt for love—now hers for confinement and shame. The knot she felt in her belly tightened; the life within her moved restlessly as if in protest.

Left alone in the dark, she pressed her fingers to her stomach and whispered, not for the elders, not for the crowd, but for the child she carried.

You are mine. The world may try to take you, but I will not let it.

Outside, Myr and Myk watched the square clear. Their faces were impassive, but in the shadowed hollows around them, ambition breathed like a secret flame. The elders had claimed victory—order had been upheld—but the price they had set would ripple outward, and none of them could say for certain whether the cost was containment or catastrophe.

CHAPTER TWELVE

TWO PRISONERS

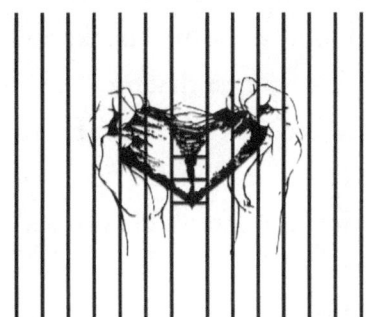

A GOODBYE

The dungeons were silent but for the drip of water and the faint hum of the wards. Two cells faced one another like mirrors of despair. Bella, chained and weary, had been thrown back into hers. Across from her lay Orin, bloodless and broken, barely more than breath and shadow.

"Orin..." Her voice was a tremor in the stillness. She pressed herself against the iron bars, reaching though she could not touch him. "My love, what have they done to you?"

There was no answer—only the ragged sound of breath. But slowly, painfully, Orin dragged himself forward, guided only by her voice. His body collapsed at last just within the reach of her fingers. Bella gathered his bloodied hand in both of hers, her tears falling to mix with the dust.

Hours passed like centuries. Orin drifted in and out of consciousness, but even broken, he tried to make himself understood. His trembling hand moved across his throat in a motion that chilled her.

"No," Bella whispered. "I will not hear it." But the motion came again. At last, the words tore from her lips, raw and anguished. "You ask me to end it?"

A faint nod. A final plea.

Her hands shook as she searched the floor, finding a discarded rope the guards had left behind. She clutched it, horrified at what it meant. "I cannot," she cried. "I cannot be the one to take you from me."

But Orin, with a gentleness that mocked his torment, pressed her hand and smiled through blood-stained lips. He took the rope, shaping it with trembling fingers, and raised himself upon a stone as if the weight of his life demanded this final act of will. He reached for her hands one last time, his touch tender even as his body failed him.

Bella begged, sobbing into the night. "Don't leave me. Please—we can find a way, we can still..."

But Orin only smiled faintly and mimed a kiss. Then he let go. The silence that followed was heavier than any roar. His body slackened, and the prison's darkness claimed him.

The world tilted. Bella fell to her knees, her cries hollow against the stone. She pressed her forehead to the bars until her skin split, whispering prayers to a Heartstone that no longer answered her.

Footsteps came. Slow, deliberate.

Jorric stood in the archway, his face cast half in shadow. He surveyed the scene—the rope, the body, the blood—with a cold curiosity.

"Well," he said softly, almost amused. "I had wondered how your little tale would end. I suppose even love stories meet their noose in time."

Bella's eyes burned, but she gave him no words. She would not give him that victory.

Jorric stepped closer, his tone sharpened. "Did you think you could hide it from me? That your betrayal would not rot its way to the surface? Perhaps you should join him now. I left the rope here for a reason, Bella. To see if you had the courage to follow your beast."

Still, she said nothing. Her silence was a blade.

Leaning close, Jorric whispered at her ear, "I know you never loved me. But you've freed me. The elders will see to it that I am rid of you, and I will live the life I was meant to."

He turned and left, his cloak brushing the stone like a funeral shroud.

Bella remained kneeling, her eyes fixed on nothing, her face carved into stillness. Something within her had died with Orin. But in the hollow, he left behind, something new awoke: a cold, vengeful fire.

The girl who had once wept for freedom was gone. In her place, a woman was forged in grief and betrayal—one who would one day make her people tremble at the name Bella Lestaire.

CHAPTER THIRTEEN

ASHES OF LOVE

MEMORIES

The cell was too quiet. Too still. The only sound Bella heard was the phantom echo of a rope swaying in her mind, though the guards had long since carried Orin's body away. She sat pressed against the bars, her dress still stiff with his blood, her hands raw from clutching at him until he slipped beyond her reach.

There were no tears left in her. The well had run dry. What remained was silence—a silence so heavy it crushed her chest with every breath. Yet within that silence, grief began to twist into something darker: fear. Fear for the child that still stirred within her.

Shadows of Memory

When she closed her eyes, Orin returned in fragments. Sometimes he was the warrior she had known, his eyes steady, his smile faint, his voice deep and soothing. Other times he came as a ruined beast, faceless and tongueless, dragging his broken body toward her in dreams that made her wake choking on her own screams.

"Live... for him."
The words rang through her mind like a whisper left behind. But was it Orin's blessing, or her own guilt shaping his voice? She did not know.

One night, exhaustion claimed her, and sleep pulled her into a vision.

She was no longer in the cell, but standing in a meadow drenched in silver moonlight. Orin stood beside her, whole and strong, his golden eyes alive with pride. In his arms he held a boy—her boy—dark-haired and laughing, reaching out for her. Bella rushed forward, her heart breaking with joy. She touched her son's small hand, and the warmth of it melted her grief for a heartbeat.

But the meadow twisted. The moon turned blood-red, the grass blackened, and chains slithered up from the soil, coiling around the boy's wrists and ankles. Orin tried to hold on, but his face began to blur, his eyes collapsing into bloody sockets. His tongue rolled from his mouth, falling at her feet.

The child screamed—not with the voice of a babe, but with the echo of wolves howling in pain. The chains dragged him into the earth, leaving Bella clawing at the soil until her nails cracked and bled.

Then a voice cut through the horror, cold and venomous. *"You cannot keep him, Bella. He belongs to us."*

Elder Myr stood where the moon had been, his smile wide, his eyes like two shards of night.

Bella awoke thrashing, her throat raw from a scream that never left her lips. The bars of her cell greeted her, and the scent of her own sweat clung to her skin. But the phantom weight of her son's hand lingered in her palm, searing her deeper than any chain.

Myr's Visit

Days later, Elder Myr himself came to the prison. He entered without a torch, his presence alone making the guards stiffen. The dim glow of ward-stones carved his lined face in shadows, and his eyes gleamed like obsidian shards. He stood at the bars, unmoving, watching Bella with a faint smile that was colder than any chain.

"You mourn him still," he said at last, his voice low, almost kindly. "Good. Grief is the chisel that shapes obedience."

Bella pressed her body tighter against the wall, clutching her belly.

Myr tilted his head, as though amused. "Do not mistake this for cruelty, child. From your womb will come a force greater than you or I. That child will not be yours. It will be the Sanctum's. It will be ours."

He turned, robes whispering against the stones, and left without another word. But his voice lingered, coiled in the corners of her mind like a serpent, tightening every time she felt the flutter of life within her.

Though her body wasted in the filth of the prison, something hardened within Bella. Her grief no longer left her limp—it coiled into her spine, braced her shoulders, sharpened her gaze. She had no plan, no means of escape, not yet. But where despair had reigned, now smoldered a spark.

They had taken Orin. They would take her child. But they would never take her love.

And in that love, a seed of rebellion stirred.

CHAPTER FOURTEEN

THE PASSING OF TIME

THE CHILD

The cell ceased to be a cage and became a tomb. Blood and fear clung to the air like damp cloth; the wards hummed a cold, endless note that made the bones ache. The spark that grief had kindled in Bella—sharp, bright, vengeful—had settled into a steady flame. Yet over and over, a heavier thought pressed its weight upon her: the child.

Orin's death—my fault. My husband betrayed. My people watching. And this life within me—what future? Will they break him to break me? If only time would stop...

Time did not stop. It advanced with cruel efficiency toward the moment when the child would draw breath.

The Birth

The hours between the trial and her labor vanished like a blink. Pains came hard and close in the cold cell. Jasper—the boy errand-runner—slopped porridge along the corridor, startled when a guard beckoned him sharply.

"Run to the Sanctum," the guard hissed. "Tell Elder Myr she's due any moment."

Jasper ran. Moments later, Myr's arrangements fell into place like stones in a wall.

"Prepare our new citizen," Myr murmured to no one and everyone. "Jasper—fetch Mora and Jina. The prison."

Mora and Jina came quickly: one thin and shy, the other stout and brisk. Between them they had delivered half the enclave's children. They entered the cell with practiced hands and empty eyes.

"We're here to help, dear," Jina said gently. "Breathe."

Bella did as she was told. She pressed her back to the stone and rode the waves. When at last the newborn cried, relief swelled—until Mora pulled a fingertip away with a hiss.

"He bit me," Mora said, incredulous. Tiny teeth. Nails too sharp for a babe. Jina flinched, then set her jaw. They both stepped back.

They dropped the child into Bella's arms. The wail stopped at once. Mother and son simply stared at each other—his eyes wide, her tears falling unbidden. For an instant, the cell was not a tomb but a hearth.

Myr's boots scraped the threshold.

"Ladies," he said smoothly. "Thank you. You will now take what is ours."

Bella clutched her child tighter. "No."

Jina hesitated, sorrow tugging at her mouth. "Forgive us," she whispered to Bella. "We must."

Mora stepped forward; Jina followed, murmuring quiet comforts that did nothing to comfort. The child was lifted away.

Myr watched Bella's arms close on emptiness. "Well done," he said, as if concluding a lesson. "Go. And keep the boy near the prison yard. I want the mother to hear him live."

The Wound That Would Not Close

Nothing compared to the pain of watching them carry her child away.

Bella unraveled slowly. Her hair dulled with grit and ash; her nails blackened with dirt as she scratched sketches into the floor—small scenes of a boy she would not see: a wooden horse, a tower of stones, a lesson whispered from mother to son.

This is crimson quartz, little one, she would murmur to the drawings. *If anyone comes to harm you, place it in your left palm and rub seven times. Your skin will burn what would touch you. A secret for us alone.*

By Myr's order, the child played in earshot of the prison—a cruelty designed to stretch her heart thin. Through the high window came peals of laughter and questions in a curious, bright voice.

"Jina, where's Mama?"

"She was taken far away to be made well," Jina lied, her voice breaking.

When sleep finally came, it dragged Bella into a world that was not freedom but fever. In the dream, her cottage was warm with sugared bread and river-scent. Orin called from the doorway: *Where is our son?* She ran into the garden—and found only the suggestion of a loss she could not face: a bloom crushed, a ribbon torn, the echo of a child's laugh swallowed by silence. The dream shifted; the voice in the doorway flattened, turned thin, became Jorric's monotone; became her father's.

Look at what you've done. Turned out just like your mother.

That last sentence shattered the dream like a thrown cup. Bella woke rigid, breath sawing, Jasper hovering uselessly at the bars.

A Name

Days ran together, but the echo of her father's words would not leave her. *Like your mother.* The phrase gnawed at the edges of her thoughts, until another voice cut through and scattered it like startled birds.

"Magistra Lycah," a boy's voice piped from the yard beyond. "This exercise is for beginners."

"Hush, Faustus," Lycah replied, crisp as winter. "Those who assume superiority die first."

Faustus.

Bella froze as the name settled into her like a warm stone. *My son is Faustus.* She tasted the syllables, and for the first time in weeks, the line of her mouth softened. She began to draw him taller in the dirt, with eyes that were neither wholly wolf nor wholly man—eyes that might one day look for her.

The Reach

The memory of her own power returned like a forgotten pulse.

Myr had tried to break her into not knowing what she was. He had succeeded—until now. Bella picked up small stones and turned them in her palm. The type didn't matter; she had always worked with instinct as much as mineral.

She reached—not with hands, but with the part of her soul that remembered the riverbeds and the Heartstone's hum. She sought Faustus, feeling for that thin, living thread that connects mother to child.

At once she struck a wall: a sterile, absolute ward, cold as iron, designed not to keep him safe but to keep *her* out. The shock made her gasp. She reached again and again. The shield repelled her each time, humming with a power that bore Myr's signature and Lycah's hand.

Fine. If she could not reach through, she would learn to reach around.

Her prison became a school. She mapped ward flows with grit and pebbles, studied pulse-falls at shift changes, counted guards and gaps, charted the exact breath when the prison's old runes guttered low. She measured time by the moon, by whispers, by musk and mildew, and she waited—not as prey, but as a hunter.

The Sanctum's Weapon

The Sanctum stripped love even from language. To the elders, the boy was not Faustus but "the anomaly."

His training was relentless: hours of stonework and sigil recitation, exercises to draw and dampen, bind and unbind. He drank moon-dulling draughts that made his senses blur and his stomach twist. Where other children were taught to steady their hands, he was taught to steady his mind until it did not flinch at pain.

Magistra Lycah taught without warmth. She did not strike him; she did not need to. Her control was the control of the blade-maker, patient and exacting. Yet in her black ink notes she recorded something she could not file away as chance.

"Elder," she said to Myr, one evening as the Heartstone throbbed low. "The boy's strength varies with the lunar cycle. He is most volatile near the full moon. Near the new, he falters."

Myr's eyes brightened, hungry. "Good. Double his herbs at the full; halve them at the new. Let us learn the measure of this tide."

He thought of the council's power, yes—but also of his own. Power was never a thing Myr wished to share.

Faustus, unaware of the calculus being done around him, obeyed. Yet the questions multiplied behind his quiet eyes. Why did the wards tilt at dusk? Why did the Heartstone hum in two notes, not one? Why did the name *Faustus* feel like a cloak, not a skin?

A New Purpose

Bella drew her son taller in the dust until the cell could no longer hold his imagined shape. She ran out of floor and started on the wall. She drew him siphoning light from sky and stone, the way she had once done in the worst of storms. As she worked, the ache inside her changed its name.

It was no longer grief alone, or fear alone.

It was purpose.

She whispered to the warded air, to the boy she could not touch: *I am coming.*

Her prison was no longer a tomb. It was a study of weaknesses, a patient rehearsal of escape. The ward hum, once a torment, became a metronome. She could feel, on certain nights, a thinning—just a hairsbreadth—where the old stone met the new rune. On those nights she slept, not from despair, but to sharpen herself for what would come.

The Sanctum thought it had forged a weapon in Faustus.

It had also, without intending, forged one in Bella Lestaire.

And one night, when moon and heartbeat and hum all came into alignment, the wards would learn the cost of mistaking a mother's love for weakness.

Chapter Fifteen

THE ESCAPE

A Warm Place

The night was cloaked in perfect darkness. The moon, absent from the sky, left the prison buried in shadow. Bella sat on the dirt floor of her cell, arms wrapped around her knees, watching her breath bloom like smoke with every exhale. The wards, she knew, were at their weakest on nights such as these—a brittle seam between the Geomancers' great rituals, when even stone whispered of weakness.

"Jasper," she said softly, her voice carrying just enough warmth to cut through the gloom.

The old guard shifted outside her cell. His hair had thinned with age, but he still clung to his duties with the rigid pride of habit. "Cold one tonight," he muttered, rubbing his hands together.

"It is," Bella agreed. "A shame you're the only one left to feel it. If the others were here, you'd take turns by the fire."

Jasper grumbled, "Aye. But I can't leave. Duty's duty."

Bella tilted her head, her gaunt face lit by a smile that seemed almost conspiratorial. "You've been here since you were a boy. You're never late, never careless. Do you think the elders care? No. But you deserve warmth, Jasper. Reward yourself. What harm could it do?"

The old man hesitated. Then, like a weary soldier surrendering to gravity, he sighed. "You're right. A quick spell by the fire, that's all."

"Take your time," Bella whispered as he walked toward the office, closing the heavy door behind him. "I'll watch the prison for you."

For the first time in years, the prison was without a guard.

The Breaking of Chains

It was not thunder, nor fire, but a whisper. Bella reached out with her mind, twisting the geomantic hum of the Heartstone that fed the wards. The lock on her cell shuddered, and with a faint click, it fell open. She froze, listening—no alarm, no footsteps. The silence held.

She slipped through the corridor like a shadow, bare feet silent on the stone. Past patrol routes she had memorized, past the guard posts where snores rose faintly. She breathed the cold air of freedom as she stepped beyond the outer wall.

The night wind struck her face, and her heart surged. She had escaped.

But freedom was not enough.

Her child was still caged within the Sanctum.

She reached the edge of the tower she had glimpsed so many times: the Sanctum, the sterile heart of Geomancer power. Its ward was visible tonight, a shimmering wall of light, pulsing with deadly energy. Soldiers stood like statues before it, their faces pale beneath their helms, weapons gleaming.

Bella's heart pounded. She could *feel* Faustus inside—his magic thrummed like a muffled heartbeat, raw and aching for her. But the ward was unbreakable. To touch it was to die.

A bitter truth sank in. She could not save him. Not yet.

Tears threatened, but she swallowed them. Turning her back, she ran.

The Edge of Despair

At the border of the settlement, the shield shimmered before her, endless and unyielding. Behind her was only torture, chains, and death. Ahead was annihilation. Perhaps, she thought, it was better. Better to end herself now than to go back.

Her heart cracked as she whispered into the night, sending her words to the wind, to her son she might never see.

"Goodbye, my son. I would have loved to raise you, to teach you all I know. But fate was not kind. Even so, never doubt this—I have always loved you."

She closed her eyes and sprinted toward the barrier.

The Explosion

In his chamber at the Sanctum, Faustus awoke to a pain that was not his own. His chest ached, his heart burned with sorrow. *This isn't mine*, he thought. *Whose pain is this?*

He pressed his hands against the window, eyes drawn to the night. In the sky, something moved—dark wings against the stars. A vampire.

Without knowing why, Faustus pushed the sorrow outward, flinging it at the creature. His untrained magic roared like a tempest.

There was a thunderous blast. Fire split the night. The vampire shrieked as it fell, burning to ash before the walls.

Faustus stumbled back, wide-eyed. "What... did I just do?"

Bella was running at full speed when the explosion shook the earth. The ward before her shattered with a flash of crimson light, just for an instant. A body plummeted from the sky, burning as it struck the ground.

She stumbled, tumbling across the dirt. When she rose, panting, she realized—she had passed through.

The shield had not killed her. She was outside.

The corpse of the vampire smoldered nearby, a grim omen. More winged shapes circled above, and shouts rose from the Sanctum. She had no time.

She fled into the forest, her breath ragged, her mind torn between anguish and fury.

The Phantom of the Woods

Behind her, the prison, the Sanctum, her son. Ahead, only darkness and exile.

She ran until her legs failed, until her lungs burned, until the forest swallowed her whole.

That night, Bella Lestaire ceased to be a daughter of the Sanctum. She became something else—an outcast, a shadow, a vengeful phantom.

The Geomancers had made her a prisoner. They had made her a widow. They had stolen her child.

Now they had created their greatest threat.

A Lonely Runner

For days, Bella ran without purpose, driven by a primal need for distance and by the cold flame of fury burning in her heart. The forest was a blur of moss and shadow, the trees standing as a silent jury to her grief. Her body, weakened by years of captivity, ached with every step, but she pressed forward still—sustained only by bitter berries, wild roots, and a will sharpened by despair.

She knew she was hunted. The Geomancers would not rest until she was dragged back to chains, and the vampires would gladly drain her for the blood they craved. Worse still, the creatures of the night had seen what her child could do—how his mere existence could unmake barriers thought eternal. Her son was a prize, a weapon, and through him, she had become an enemy to all.

By the third day, as the sun sank into a bleeding horizon, her strength failed. She collapsed beneath a fallen log, curling into herself like a wounded animal. The forest pressed close with its silence, and for the first time since her escape, Bella felt the crushing weight of futility. She had failed her child. She had abandoned him. She was a mother who had forsaken her only reason to live.

A hollow laugh broke from her cracked lips.

"Ha... look at you, Bella. A pitiful ghost. Running away from your child, running away from death. And now you will die here, like a starving animal."

Her own voice answered, sharp, unforgiving:

"No—you are not dying here. You are running, yes, but running from yourself. That child is yours, and you left him. What kind of mother does that make you?"

Her tears fell hot against the cold earth. "You're right," she whispered. "I am a terrible mother."

But another voice rose from the hollow of her mind, gentler, almost merciful. *"No. You are not a bad mother. You simply never had one to show you how. And your father—your father chained your heart before you could even choose to love."*

The thought shattered as the forest stirred. A faint rustle. A heavy tread. Bella's instincts sharpened. She glimpsed movement at the corner of her vision—something more than a bat's wings, too purposeful to be the aimless stirrings of night. She froze. *Vampire?*

But then the shadow emerged from the trees. Not gliding with the cruel elegance of a vampire but walking with the steady weight of a seasoned hunter. A man—tall, broad-shouldered, a gray-streaked beard across a weathered face carved from stone. He bore a staff of ironwood, and over his shoulders hung a cloak of buck hide, worn with age. His eyes, deep as rich earth, burned not with menace, but with sorrow.

"You are not of the forest, little bird," he rumbled, his voice low as distant thunder. He did not demand answers, nor ask what she was, nor why she ran. He simply extended a hand. "You are broken. Let me help you."

Bella's heart hammered. His presence was too certain, too knowing. The Sanctum's wards should have hidden her existence from all. She recoiled instinctively, trained by years of cruelty to expect only pain. Yet when her gaze met his, she felt not fear but a strange, shattering familiarity. His touch, when she accepted his hand, was warm. Familiar.

Her breath trembled. "Do... do I know you?"

The man's only answer was silence. He guided her gently to her feet and led her through the forest to a cave hidden behind woven vines and stone. A fire flickered within, its light dancing over the rough walls. He gave her dried venison, a skin of water, and said nothing until she had eaten. His silence was steady, comforting, like the presence of someone who had seen too much of the world to be hurried.

At last, he spoke. "The Geomancers seek you. And the vampires are hunting as well. They search for a resonance they do not understand. They search for your child."

Bella's lips parted. Her mind reeled. *How does he know?* She clutched her hands tight, her heart racing. "What do you mean?" she pressed. "What is my child capable of?"

The man only gave her a long, sad smile. His silence was heavier than words.

"How do you know all of this?" she whispered.

His dark eyes glimmered with grief. He reached beneath his cloak and revealed a crude carving hung on a leather thong—a wolf, simple and unfinished. He held it as one holds a relic of the dead.

"I know because I felt it," he said at last, his voice cracking into a growl. "Wolves can smell life, but we can smell death as well. I felt it when he died. My son. My Orin."

The name was a knife to her chest. Bella's breath caught; her world tipped sideways. She saw again the scars on Orin's chest, his hands on hers, the sound of his voice whispering love through iron bars. And now, staring into this man's eyes, she saw the same fire—older, tempered by loss, but undeniable.

She whispered the truth her heart already knew. "You are his father."

The man bowed his head. "My name is Emor," he said. "I was an alpha once. A leader. A father who could not save his son. And now..." His voice grew heavy, like stone grinding against stone. "Now I am a grandfather. And I will not let my child's child be chained, tortured, or used. Not by Geomancer, not by vampire. Not by anyone."

Bella's tears fell freely. For the first time since Orin's death, she felt the stirrings of something other than despair. Hope—but a fierce, dangerous hope. She had found an ally. A father bound by blood to the man she loved.

Emor's gaze bore into hers, unyielding. "We will save the boy, Bella Lestaire. But hear me: if you falter, if you fail him, I will finish what the elders began. For Orin's blood, for Faustus's future."

And in that moment, under the shadow of wolves and the cold gaze of the moon, a new alliance was forged—not of trust, but of necessity.

CHAPTER SIXTEEN

DESPERATE ALLIANCE

THE WOLFPACK

B ella's body was frail, her legs trembling with each step, but with Emor's steady hand guiding her, she endured. The fire in her heart had returned, burning with one thought alone: Faustus.

"We must find them," Bella said, her voice raw with desperation. "Your pack. They are the only ones who can help us."

Emor's face darkened, his grief-lined eyes narrowing into steel. "My pack is not what it once was. The Geomancers have scattered us like ashes. And the new alpha—Terrek—he is no leader. He is a brute who worships violence and despises mercy. He calls kindness the weakness that killed my son."

He stepped to the mouth of the cave, staring into the shifting shadows of the forest as if it were an enemy he had long been at war with. "But you are right. They are all that remains. We do not go to them as beggars. We go with a warning: the humans have forged a weapon beyond their control. The vampires hunt for it as well. If the pack does not understand the truth, they will all be slaughtered."

Bella's breath caught. She hesitated, then asked the question that had burned in her mind since their first meeting. "Emor... something you said before. You said *we all saw what my son was capable of.* What did you mean?"

Emor turned slowly, his face grave. "You were there that night. You fell. You ran headlong toward the Geomancer's shield. We thought you would burn where you stood. We thought your body would shatter like glass." He stepped closer, his voice low and steady. "But you did not. The barrier fell aside. And a vampire fell with it. Do you think that was your doing? No. It was him. The boy. My grandson. He saved you."

Bella's eyes widened. Her lips parted, but no sound came.

Emor let the silence stretch, then added: "We do not know how. We do not know why. But it was his will that broke the shield."

Her mind spun. She felt dizzy with revelation, with terror, with hope. Yet suspicion pierced her, sharp and cold. She narrowed her eyes. "Why were you watching the Geomancers? Watching my son?"

A sad smile curved Emor's lips. He knew the doubt in her heart. "We scout them every full moon. The vampires, the Sanctum, the humans—always. For it is the one night our power rises to its peak. On those nights, we saw a child in the Sanctum performing feats no child could. Feats that rivaled Myr himself. And we knew—only one bloodline could have birthed such a thing." His eyes glistened, the firelight catching in their depths. "We knew Orin's son lived. My grandson."

Bella felt the words strike her like blows. She had no answer. No strength left to argue.

Emor placed a hand on her shoulder, heavy with sorrow and promise. "Rest now, little bird. Tomorrow, we walk into the den of wolves. And you will need all your strength."

And Bella, exhausted, closed her eyes. Sleep came quickly, merciful and dark.

The Forest Memory

When she awoke, the sun was pale in the sky, giving no warmth. They traveled deeper into the woods, where the air smelled of pine and the shadows thickened. The scent struck Bella like an arrow to memory.

She was a child again, running to keep pace with her father. "Where are we going?" she had asked, breathless.

"You'll see," Loryndor had replied, eager as a boy. He had led her to the northern woods—lands forbidden and dangerous, but untouched by vampire or werewolf.

At last, he climbed a tree, reaching for a nest he had spied days before. "Close your eyes, Bella," he said, smiling. But when he looked inside, his face fell. The nest was empty. On the ground lay a fledgling—its wing broken, its tiny body trembling in its last breaths.

Bella gasped. "Oh no, father—what did you do?"

"I did nothing," Loryndor muttered. "The mother abandoned it. I thought you might care for it, but..." His voice trailed off.

Bella scooped the bird against her chest, tears in her eyes. "There, little one. You will be fine."

And then, impossibly, the bird stirred. It chirped once, weakly, then with sudden strength. It stretched its wings and rose into the sky.

Loryndor's face went pale. He seized Bella's hand. "Let's go."

"Why? I want to find more birds!" she had protested.

But he only muttered, darkly: "It cannot be. Not like her." His eyes clouded, and when they returned home, his smile never came back.

The memory broke as Bella stumbled on a root. She blinked, and the forest pressed in once more—darker, colder, filled with the low growls of waiting predators.

The Pack

At last, they reached the edge of the pack's land. The moon rose pale and thin, and the air grew heavy with the scent of wolf and blood. A growl echoed through the trees, soon joined by others, until the forest rumbled with menace.

Emor stepped forward, shoulders squared, hand on the wolf carving around his neck. His voice cut through the night. "It is I, Emor. Once alpha of this pack. I return not in power, but with a warning. A new war is upon us."

From the shadows came hulking shapes, their eyes burning like coals. Wolves, half-man and half-beast, scarred and ragged from endless battles. They encircled the pair, fangs bared, fur bristling.

A voice broke from the dark, mocking. "You still live, old man? I thought the earth had swallowed you long ago." The speaker stepped forward—a massive figure, fur streaked with gray, his jaw scarred from countless fights. Terrek, the new alpha. His voice dripped contempt. "What do you want? And who is this?" His gaze fixed on Bella, sharp as a knife.

"I come not to beg," Emor said, unflinching. "But to warn. The Geomancers have bred a weapon beyond reckoning. The vampires circle like vultures. If we do nothing, we will all be destroyed."

Terrek sneered. "And you bring *this*—a human witch—to my den? Did you forget, old wolf, who slaughtered our kin? Do you think your son died because of strength? No. He died because of weakness. *Your* weakness."

Bella stepped forward, her voice steady despite her shaking hands. "My name is Bella. I bring you knowledge you cannot afford to ignore."

Terrek bared his teeth, towering over her. "I should tear your throat here and now. Let your blood stain these woods as warning."

Emor moved between them, his presence like a wall of iron. "She is not the enemy. The child is. A child born of mage and wolf. My grandson. Her son. If we do not act, he will destroy us all—or worse, be enslaved to destroy us."

The pack shifted uneasily, low growls rumbling through their ranks. Terrek's face twitched with doubt, but he snarled it away. "A child? You dare spin tales of babes while our blood soaks the earth? I hear nothing but weakness."

Bella's voice cut sharp through the growls. "It is Orin's child. Your brother's blood. His power is already greater than yours. Do nothing, and he will be your doom."

The pack fell into silence. Fear glimmered in their eyes, but Terrek barked a cruel laugh to drown it. "Lies. The whining of the broken and the weak. Get out, both of you. Leave, or I'll finish what the humans could not."

His pack howled with him, their voices rising like a storm.

Emor placed a hand on Bella's arm. Without a word, they turned their backs and walked into the shadows of the forest, leaving the growls and hatred of the pack behind.

CHAPTER SEVENTEEN

A VOICE FROM THE PAST

THE BROTHER

T he moon was a pale, watchful eye above the forest, thin and sharp as a blade. The air carried the musk of wolf and the copper tang of old blood. Bella and Emor had barely set foot on the edge of the pack's domain when the night erupted with growls. From every shadow, shapes emerged—half-man, half-beast, their bodies scarred, their eyes burning like coals in the dark. The forest trembled with menace.

Emor stepped forward, broad shoulders squared, his hand resting on the wolf carving that hung from his neck. His voice was deep, steady, cutting cleanly through the snarls.

"I am Emor, once Alpha of this pack. I return not for power, but with warning. A new war rises, and it will not spare us."

The wolves closed in, a circle of bristling fur and gleaming fangs. From among them stepped a hulking figure, fur streaked with gray, jaw marked by an old scar that cut across his face like a lightning strike. His presence was raw dominance, his eyes hard and cruel.

"Still, you live, old man?" Terrek, the new alpha, sneered, his voice dripping with mockery. "I thought the earth had claimed your bones. And yet you return—with a human?" His gaze fell on Bella, sharp as a dagger's point.

"I come not to beg," Emor said, unflinching before the growls of the pack. "But to warn. The Geomancers forge a weapon greater than their stones, greater than their wards. And the vampires circle like vultures, waiting to strike. If we do nothing, if we fight one another instead of what is coming, there will be nothing left for wolves, mages, or men."

Terrek barked a harsh laugh, teeth flashing in the moonlight. "And you bring this witch to my den to preach doom? Do you forget who slaughtered our kin? Do you forget your son's death? He died not of their strength, but of your weakness."

Bella stepped forward, though her knees trembled beneath her. "My name is Bella. I do not come to deceive you. I come with knowledge you cannot afford to ignore."

The wolves snarled as one, but Terrek only leaned closer, towering over her, his hot breath sharp as iron. "I should tear your throat where you stand and let your blood soak this soil as warning to the rest of your kind."

Before Bella could answer, Emor moved, a wall of iron between them. His voice rang with a fire that had once commanded the pack. "She is not the enemy. The child is. A child born of mage and wolf. My grandson. Her son. If we do not act, he will either destroy us—or be enslaved to destroy us."

The pack faltered, low growls turning uncertain. Fear glimmered in their eyes, though Terrek's snarl grew sharper.

"A child?" he spat. "You dare spin such weakness in front of me? The humans break us with stone and fire, not with babes in swaddling cloth."

Bella's voice struck like steel on stone. "It is Orin's child. Your brother's blood runs in him. His power has already eclipsed yours. Do nothing, and he will be your doom."

For a heartbeat, silence fell. Even the forest stilled. The name of Orin carried weight, even among wolves hardened by hatred. Some lowered their eyes, haunted by memory. Terrek's lip curled, fighting the unease with rage.

"Lies," he barked, though his voice lacked its former certainty. "The weak cling to stories, the broken to ghosts. I hear nothing but madness. Leave, both of you—or I'll finish what the humans could not."

The pack howled with him, a storm of sound, wild and merciless.

Emor placed a steady hand on Bella's arm. Without another word, they turned and walked back into the shrouded forest, the wolves' fury echoing behind them.

But as they reached the edge of the clearing, the howls faltered. A voice rolled across the night, low and resonant, neither wolf nor man.

"Blood of wolf and mage... do not spurn it, or it will be your ruin."

The sound hung in the trees like smoke. The pack froze. Terrek's eyes darted through the shadows, fury flashing into doubt. Some swore the voice was Orin's, others the echo of an ancient Heartstone buried deep beneath the forest. Whatever it was, it carried a weight no wolf could dismiss.

Bella's heart clenched, for she knew that voice. It was the same whisper that had haunted her dreams—the ghost of the man she had loved.

Emor's face was unreadable, but his voice was hushed when he finally spoke. "The past still speaks. And the pack will not forget."

An Unlikely Council

Bryn's fury had cooled into something harder than grief—a stone set in the center of him that would not be softened. He stood by the cave mouth, the firelight carving his jaw into planes of shadow. When he spoke, his voice was lower, measured.

"Bella," he said, "I want to apologize for my first cruelty. I mourned like a blind thing. My brother... he loved with no boundaries. He would have shown mercy to a vampire if it came to it. I... I spoke before I thought."

Bella looked up. In Bryn's eyes she saw Orin—those same hazel depths that had haunted her dreams. She said nothing; her chin dropped as if the sight cost her something.

Bryn no longer saw her as traitor but as casualty—an instrument of the same wound that had taken his brother. The calculating intelligence in his gaze had not dulled; it had sharpened. "We cannot blunder," he said. "We must move like bone through water—silent and exact. No innocents may be harmed. You," he turned to Emor, "you will not charge like a fool. And you," his eyes cut to Bella, "you must tell us how to get your boy. You are the key."

Emor's hand tightened on the crude wolf-carving at his throat. "I will not hide while my grandson is bred into a thing for the Geomancers' shelves," he said, voice coiled with old authority. "I will not let another child be stolen from me."

Terrek's shadow still lurked at the edge of memory—his brute force and fury—yet here, in the hush after the pack's snarls, a quieter urgency held them. Bryn's plan took shape not from bravado but from necessity.

"The Sanctum is not a gate you batter with teeth," Bella said softly, her voice steady despite the ache in her limbs. "Its wards are sympathetic—mirrors of the Geomancers' minds. They read intent. They burn what is foreign. A recklessly led charge will be ash before the courtyard gates open."

Bryn listened, grinding his teeth once. "So, we must become ghosts in their halls," he said. "Not wolves at all."

"No," Bella corrected. "Not wolves. Resonance. I cannot make you mages. I will not make you what you are not. But I can graft a temporary signature—an echo of Geomancer thought—onto your bodies. The wards will mistake you for kin long enough to pass. It is sympathetic trickery, not transformation. The cost is endurance; the signature fades with time. We have to move like a whisper."

Emor nodded. The fire reflected in his eyes, and for a moment he looked twelve years younger—an alpha who had not yet learned sorrow. "So we walk among them as their shadow."

"Precisely," Bella said, pressing her finger into the dirt and drawing a crude map. Her movements were careful, almost ritualistic. "The outer wards are a lattice. They loop and answer one another. There is a changing of the guard—an eclipse in the weave—every six hours. That is the seam we must thread. We step through when the wards are distracted, when the Heartstone's heartbeat wanes for a breath."

Bryn crouched to study the map, the lines catching in his eyes. "And once inside?"

"Silence," Bella said. "The Sanctum listens. Its corridors carry sound like wind carries scent. You move with the shadow. You do not strike unless I call it. I will lead us on the sympathetic thread—Faustus is an ember in the weave. He will tug at the signature; I will feel him. We find him. We take him. We leave the same way we came, before the signature bleeds out."

Emor's gaze was all hunger and hope. "And if the vampires are there first?"

"Then we do not reach Faustus at all," Bella answered bluntly. "They will not return empty-handed. They will carry him away into darkness that even you may not rip open. We cannot allow that to happen."

Bryn's jaw hardened. He rose to his full height, the cave shadows making him look taller, more imposing. "Then we move fast. No hesitations. No quarrels. We do this for the child, not for the woman who bore him."

Bella met his stare without flinching. "Agreed." Her voice was a quiet vow.

Bryn's lips curled. "Do not take my words for forgiveness," he warned. "This is blood, not reconciliation. But blood keeps its own counsel. We do what must be done."

They set the plan in the embers' glow like a surgeon set a scalpel. A mother, a broken alpha, and a son turned to steel—an alliance forged in ruin and sharpened by necessity. No heraldry bound them, no vows of kinship; only one raw, unassailable objective: to rescue Faustus before the Sanctum or the vampires turned him into a weapon none could stand against.

The map in the dirt lay between them, lines and circles and shaded paths. Bella traced the route once more, feeling the old rhythms of Geomancy return like a tide. She felt the wards as a faint pulse beneath her fingertips—heard the echo of the Heartstone as if it were a heartbeat far away. Hope felt thin, but for the first time since Orin's death, it felt like something actionable—like a blade ready to be wielded.

Bryn crouched beside her and, softer than before, said, "Then we begin at dusk. Rest now. We move when the wards blink."

Emor's hand fell on Bella's shoulder—heavy, protective. "Sleep, little bird. We will bring him home."

She let the words be the small warmth she clung to, then laid her head back against the cave wall and closed her eyes. Outside, the forest held its breath, as if the trees themselves anticipated the coming storm.

The Echo of Stone and Blood

The fire in Emor's cave had burned low, the embers glowing like sleeping eyes. Bella drew a circle in the dirt, her fingers trembling with both exhaustion and purpose. At the circle's edge she placed stones she had gathered—each one humming with the faint resonance of the Heartstone.

"Sit," she said quietly. "Both of you. If this is to work, your blood must carry the echo of their power."

Bryn scowled. "If you mean we must play at being Geomancers, I'll tell you now—I'll spit it out before I swallow it."

Bella did not rise to his bait. Her voice was calm, deliberate. "It is not about obedience. It is about resonance. You do not become them—you only wear their shadow for a short time. But the wards cannot be fooled by flesh alone. They will taste your blood, your heartbeat, your breath. They will look for what is not theirs."

Emor lowered himself into the circle with a solemn weight, his gray cloak spilling over his broad shoulders. "Then give me the shadow, girl," he said. "I will wear whatever lie is needed to reach him."

Bella placed her hands on the stones, her eyes closing. She whispered the old syllables of sympathetic magic, her voice a low, thrumming song that made the air vibrate. The stones began to glow faintly, pulsing in time with her heartbeat.

"Give me your hand," she said.

Emor extended his. Bella pricked his palm with a sharp shard of quartz. His blood spilled dark into the dust, and she smeared it across the stone. The glow flared, then sank into his skin. Emor shuddered as if ice had run through his veins.

"What do you feel?" Bella asked.

Emor's jaw tightened. "As though my bones have been set to ringing. Every breath tastes of stone. But... the wards. I can feel them. Faint, like thunder far away."

Bryn scoffed but offered his hand all the same. "Do it," he said.

She cut him too, his blood hissing on the quartz. When the glow entered him, Bryn hissed and shook his head violently. "This feels wrong," he growled. "Like I'm wearing a dead man's skin."

Bella's eyes snapped open. "That is exactly what it is. A borrowed skin. A false note in a song. You must bear it or you will burn before the gate."

Bryn clenched his fist, swallowing his fury. "Then I will bear it."

For long moments the three sat in silence, the glow of the stones slowly fading back into earth. Bella leaned back, her body trembling with strain. "It will hold for only a few hours at a time," she warned. "Any longer, and the wards will taste the lie and tear it apart. We must time our strike with precision."

Emor looked to her, then to Bryn. His voice was low, but it carried the weight of command. "Then we move at dusk tomorrow. When the guards change, when the wards blink. That is our window."

Bryn nodded reluctantly, hazel eyes glinting in the firelight. "If this fails, we die. If it works... we walk as ghosts in the lion's den."

Bella let her gaze fall to the dirt map, to the crude lines marking the Sanctum. Her voice was a whisper, almost to herself. "Not ghosts. Shadows. Shadows that will steal back what was stolen."

The fire guttered once, sending sparks into the dark. Outside, the forest groaned with wind, as though the world itself listened to their pact.

CHAPTER EIGHTEEN

THE NEW CONTAINMENT PROTOCOL

THE COUNCILS'S DELIBERATION

Faustus's world was carved from silence and stone. His life had been a cycle of drills, lessons, and chains that bound not just his body but his very spirit. Yet at night, when the moon pulled at the hidden part of him, the silence cracked.

The beast within paced in dreams. He ran through endless forests, his throat aching with an unvoiced howl, his hands warped into claws, the moon a predator that hunted him.

And always—always—when the terror threatened to consume him, something pierced through. A thread. A voice.

It was not the harsh chant of a Geomancer, nor the calculated cruelty of an elder. It was a lullaby, faint as breath on glass. A melody without words, soft and sorrowful, carrying the warmth of hearth-fire and clean water. Sometimes it came with the faintest fragrance—the smell of crushed petals, roses mixed with damp earth. He did not know what it was, but it cut through the storm.

He woke each time with his heart hammering, the memory already dissolving like mist, but leaving behind an ache he could not name.

When Magistra Lycah gave him the Lunar Elixir and bound him in Heartstones, he writhed as always, his veins burning, his mind caged. Yet deep within, behind the screams, the lullaby stirred again. *There, there. Don't cry.* The words were never spoken aloud, yet he felt them. Felt them more keenly than the chains.

The boy didn't know if it was a memory, a dream, or a trick. But it frightened the Geomancer within him, and it strengthened the boy.

Project Tethering

The council of Geomancers convened beneath the Sanctum's vaulted dome, its walls alive with etched wards that pulsed faintly in rhythm with the Heartstone buried deep below. Their voices, though hushed, throbbed with urgency, each word a tremor of fear.

Magistra Lycah's revelation weighed on them like a curse: *The boy is no anomaly. He is a new magic. A fusion of moon and stone. Lunar Geomancy.*

Mage Monarch Delani's face, sharp as a dagger's edge, twitched with fury. Yet even he could not deny what the shattered stones in Faustus's chamber had proven. Suppression had failed. The Elixirs no longer bound him. The wards cracked at his scream.

So they turned to a last resort, their whispers settling into a single name: Project Tethering.

The Alpha Heartstone would be the anchor; a relic dragged from the ruins of the First City. It throbbed not with creation, but with the still, terrible silence of death. To bind Faustus to it would be to shackle his life to an ocean of endings. His howl would become their shield. His body, their fortress.

But it would require pain—pain so sharp it split the mind into submission. A new elixir of silver, moon herbs, and serpent venom. Not a draught of fog, but of clarity. A poison that would scour every thought raw until he was pliant enough to accept the tether.

Their weapon would no longer be a boy. He would be a living Heartstone, their triumph and their captive.

Faustus's Sensing

In his chamber, far above the council hall, Faustus sat by the narrow window, the pale slice of moon barely visible through the wards. His hands trembled, though with what—fear or fury—he could not say.

He felt it again. That pulse. Not the steady rhythm of his own magic, but something colder, deeper, crawling beneath the earth like a buried leviathan. It thrummed in his bones, slow and heavy, as if the world itself was dragging chains across his soul.

They were planning something. He could not hear their words, but he tasted their fear, bitter and metallic in the back of his throat.

And through it all—the echo of her voice. The woman from his dreams. The one who called him *son*. The memory of her cry still gnawed at the edges of his mind, louder than the chants, stronger than the Elixirs.

They fear me. They hide truths. They build prisons I cannot see.

He clenched his fists until his nails cut crescents into his palms. The beast stirred, restless. The moon above was a thin blade, but it still carved at him, pulling, promising.

Faustus whispered to the night, his breath fogging the glass. "They think they can chain me. They will try. But I will break them. All of them."

The Council's Final Word

Down in the antechamber, the decision hardened. The vote was unanimous. The ritual would proceed.

Project Tethering.

The boy would no longer belong to himself. He would be the Sanctum's ward, their shield against vampire and wolf alike. They would forge him into stone, and if his soul screamed, so much the better.

Mage Monarch Delani raised his staff, the air hissing with runes. "So, it is decreed. Prepare the Alpha Heartstone. Brew the Elixir. The boy is no longer child nor beast. He is our weapon, and tomorrow—" his voice sharpened into steel "—we bind him."

CHAPTER NINETEEN

A SANCTUM'S DESPERATE GAMBLE

A WEAPON OR CHAOS?

The Sanctum—fortress of cold logic, built on bedrock and arrogance—had never known fear. Yet after the failed ritual, fear seeped into its stone like frost. The chamber where Faustus had been bound lay in ruins. The three Heartstones, once the unyielding anchors of their control, were not merely cracked but shattered, their sigils dim, their resonance dead. No Geomancer could remember such a thing happening.

Faustus was gone—not physically, but metaphysically. His body remained in the Sanctum, yet his mind had slipped the leash. His psychic echo, once a faint hum the elders could predict and suppress, now roared like a storm through the walls of their fortress. He had not broken free of their control; he had broken the concept of control itself. The boy was no longer a project or a weapon. He was a cataclysm.

The Council Convenes

In the central chamber, beneath the great, ancient Heartstone that powered their stronghold, the Council gathered. Their faces were pale, lips thin, voices low. Even these masters of cold calculation could not hide the truth: they had created something they could not kill.

Elder Myr stood silent, his sharp eyes betraying little, though his mind burned with old, unspoken fears. Magistra Lycah, who had overseen the rituals, entered last. She bore the look of a woman who had stared into a storm and chosen not to flinch.

The elder whose face was as dry and cracked as parchment spoke first. "The anomaly. What is its status?"

Lycah's tone was clinical, though her words trembled with a terrible certainty.

"The subject, Faustus, has exceeded every projection. The lunar current we have long suppressed is no longer separate from his Geomancy—it has become its amplifier. He is not bound by his curse; he is its master. He is a nexus of power. We cannot contain him. We cannot kill him. If we try, the backlash will reduce this Sanctum to rubble."

The chamber went silent. The truth was heavier than stone.

A Fire to Direct

"So," another elder growled, "we have forged the very blight we sought to prevent. A creature of chaos, a doom to us all."

"No," Lycah said sharply, her eyes glittering with a dangerous light. "Not a doom. An opportunity."

They turned to her. Her voice hardened into steel.

"We cannot suppress him. But we can use him. A fire uncontrolled consumes all—but a fire directed? It destroys our enemies first. The vampires circle like carrion. The wolves gather in desperation. Let them come. We will draw them here."

A murmur rose among the council. To deliberately weaken their wards, to *invite* their enemies, was madness. Yet madness was all they had left.

Lycah pressed on. "We will broadcast his resonance. We will leave a seam in the wards, just wide enough for them to believe they have broken us. They will come to claim the child. And when they are before our gates, when they are within reach..." She placed her pale hand upon the central Heartstone. "We will tether Faustus not to suppression, but to this. We will amplify him. Through the Heartstone, his storm will become a weapon vast enough to obliterate all who stand against us. A Geomantic apocalypse—directed, not endured."

The Dice are Cast

The elders exchanged long, silent glances. Survival was their law. Ruthlessness their creed. They did not hesitate long.

"So be it," croaked the parchment-faced elder. "We will risk annihilation for the certainty of annihilating others first."

The chamber grew darker as the Heartstone itself began to shift. Faint cracks of light crawled across its surface, the first signs of a gamble no Geomancer in history had dared.

Myr alone stood apart, his hands clasped behind his back. Outwardly, he gave no sign of dissent. But inside, an old fear twisted. He remembered another child, long ago—Bella. He remembered her power blooming from kindness, a thing no Geomancer could replicate. If her son had inherited even a spark of that... then the council was not amplifying a fire. They were uncaging a storm that would burn them all.

The Beacon

In the nights that followed, the wards of the Sanctum shifted. To the untrained, it seemed a faltering defense. To the wolves and the vampires who scouted the borders, it looked like weakness. But in truth, it was an invitation—a deliberate seam, a silent call.

And woven through it all, Faustus's psychic roar pulsed outward into the world. It was not merely power; it was a beacon.

The dice had been thrown. The trap was set. The Sanctum, once unshakable, now gambled with apocalypse.

Chapter Twenty

THE BEACON

The Wolf and the Witch

F ar from Emor's cave, across the rivers where the fog clung heavy and the soil reeked of old blood, the vampires stirred.

In the heart of a crumbling citadel, where the stone was blackened by centuries of moonless rites, a council gathered. They were not bound by thrones or ceremony, but by hunger and instinct. Their eyes, red as coals, snapped open all at once. They had felt it.

The eldest among them, a towering figure draped in a cloak of shredded silk, raised a clawed hand for silence. His voice slithered through the chamber like smoke.

"You feel it," he whispered. "The beacon. A song in the marrow. A child born of wolf and witch."

The younger vampires shifted, hissing, their fangs glinting in the torchlight. One snarled, "It is not a song. It is a challenge. He calls to us. A new blood, stronger than ours, stronger than theirs. If he is not claimed, he will be our doom."

The eldest smiled, revealing a mouth of perfect ivory fangs. "Not claimed, little one. Tethered. Harnessed. A wolf howls at the moon, but a vampire bends it to shadow." His gaze turned toward the east, toward the Sanctum. "The Geomancers think themselves clever. They broadcast their weapon as bait. But bait feeds not the hunter. It feeds the predator who waits in silence."

A murmur rippled through the council—low, eager, hungry.

"Then it begins," another voice rasped, high and thin, like dry parchment tearing. "The war of three. The wolves will answer the call, the humans prepare the snare, and we..." His eyes glittered with a terrible hunger. "...we will take the prize for ourselves."

The citadel erupted into whispers and growls, a chorus of blood-lust and anticipation. To the vampires, the beacon was not a warning. It was a summons. An invitation to claim the single most precious bloodline in the world.

The moon hung low and pale over their fortress as the council dispersed into the night. The air filled with the beating of countless wings, their shadows spilling across the land like a tide of death.

The hunt had begun.

CHAPTER TWENTY-ONE

THE RACE TO THE SANCTUM

A MOTHER, A BROKEN ALPHA, AND A VENGEFUL SON

The forest, once a familiar landscape of shadows and scents, had transformed into a gauntlet of death. Every tree seemed to lean closer; every rustle carried the promise of pursuit. The beacon of Faustus's power was no longer a faint hum—it was a screaming tempest that split the night, guiding friend and foe alike to the same inevitable clash.

Bryn ran ahead, a blur of muscle and shadow, his keen senses sweeping every shift in the air. He was more than a scout—he was the knife's edge between survival and slaughter. His nose twitched at the faintest scents: the sweat of men, the musk of wolves, the copper sting of vampire hunger. His body was taut, ready to strike or vanish at a moment's warning.

Emor remained at Bella's side, his ironwood staff a silent pillar of strength. He moved slower than his son once had, but no less fierce, his presence grounding her in the chaos. For Bella, every breath was war. Her Geomancy surged like a second heart, pulling her into the earth, into the old wards and snares the Geomancers had sown through the forest. A tilt of her hand, a whisper of warning, and Emor would adjust their stride, Bryn would swerve wide. She was no longer weaving hearth charms or guiding crops to bloom—she was unraveling the map of her enemy's mind.

The alliance of the three—mother, broken alpha, vengeful son—was fragile, but necessity bound them with steel.

They pressed deeper, where the old border lay between wolf and man, a place once marked with blood and fire. The beacon tugged harder here, each pulse in Bella's skull threatening to drive her to her knees.

Suddenly Bryn froze, his hand raised like a blade. The forest around them seemed to hold its breath. His nose lifted, and his lips peeled back in a low snarl.

"Not men," he growled, his voice barely more than a whisper of thunder. "Vampires. A hunting party. They're ahead of us. Moving fast. Toward the Sanctum."

Bella's stomach turned cold. Her voice cracked. "If they reach him first..."

"They'll fall into the trap," Emor said grimly, eyes hard as stone. "And when they do, the Geomancers will unleash him."

The thought twisted through them like a knife: Faustus, no longer just a child, no longer just Bella's son—he was the Sanctum's weapon. And if unleashed, he would not distinguish between vampire, wolf, or human.

A Shared Resolve

The three of them exchanged no promises, no empty words. The time for grief, for doubt, for vengeance would come later—if there was a later. Now there was only the race.

They tightened their pace. Bryn darted forward, muscles coiled like a predator in full pursuit. Emor pressed harder, his staff digging into the soil to propel his aging body further. Bella's heart hammered with each stride, her Geomancy flaring in sparks that guided them around wards, across traps, through the cracks of the forest's hostile embrace.

No longer fugitives. No longer mourners.

They were racing against wolves. Against vampires. Against men.

And against the ticking clock of the apocalypse itself.

The beacon burned brighter, its call undeniable. Ahead, beyond the trees, the Sanctum waited—not as salvation, but as executioner.

The night had become a battlefield, and the first clash had already begun.

CHAPTER TWENTY-TWO

THE VAMPIRE'S AWAKENING

VAMPIRE HIERARCHY

In the heart of a ruined cathedral, where stained glass lay shattered and the great bells had long since fallen to dust, the court of the vampires gathered. The vaulted arches dripped with moss and shadow, the air heavy with the scent of old stone and older blood. At the center, upon a throne carved from black obsidian and bleached bone, sat Count Arad DeLavoit, lord of the eternal night. His golden chalice brimmed with blood-wine, and his amber eyes glimmered with the cold patience of one who had seen centuries crumble like ash.

The hall was silent but for the echo of dripping water and the faint, restless hiss of the gathered vampires. Then the silence fractured. A resonance shivered through the walls—high-pitched, wild, a dissonant scream of power that did not belong to humans or wolves. The cathedral itself seemed to tremble with it, ancient stone answering to the call.

Arad stilled, his chalice hovering in his hand. For the first time in centuries, his lips curved into something resembling a smile. It was not joy, but recognition. A new force had been born.

From the line of kneeling courtiers, one figure stepped forward. Rosianna Holt—once a farmer's wife, now centuries a creature of the night—bowed low. Her dark eyes, twin black pearls, flickered with unease.

"My lord," she whispered, her voice quaking though her body did not. "The resonance... it comes from the humans' Sanctum. It is raw, uncontrolled. Not crafted. Not wielded. It is... unleashed."

Her mind returned, as it always did when confronted with chaos, to the night of her own making. She had gone from laughter and festival lanterns to blood-slicked teeth in the span of a heartbeat, a horse slain beneath her, her children gone before dawn. She had wept until her tears turned crimson, and in that grief, Count Arad had found her—broken, hungry, and willing to serve. Now she trembled again, as if the echo of that first transformation whispered through this new beacon.

A Lord's Cold Revelation

Arad rose, tall and terrible, his frame casting a shadow that seemed to stretch beyond the ruined hall. His voice, when it came, was a silken growl that rolled like thunder against the cracked stones.

"Raw. Untamed." He savored the words like vintage blood. "The Geomancers, in their arrogance, have opened a wound in the earth itself. And what bleeds from it is not their magic, not their order, but something older. Something they cannot bind."

He paced to the edge of the dais; his amber eyes turned toward the horizon where the Sanctum brooded. "We have always known of their wolf-child. Always known of the weapon they tried to forge. But their wards, their walls, were strong. Impenetrable. Until now."

He raised his chalice in mockery, a toast to the inevitable. "The cage is broken. The beacon is lit. And the prize is calling to us."

The court stirred, whispers like dry leaves on stone. Hunting parties—lean, starved predators draped in rags and jewels alike—shifted eagerly in the shadows.

Arad's voice cut them still.

"The child is no longer a prisoner. He is a key. A weapon of both wolf and mage. The Geomancers wish to use him as a shield. We will make him our sword. Imagine it: their wards torn down, their Sanctum ashes, the werewolf packs scattered like dogs before the hunt. Dominion—absolute, eternal."

His smile widened, fangs glinting like ivory daggers. "This is the night we have waited for. The wolves are broken. The humans are desperate. The Geomancers, in their terror, have lit a fire they cannot contain. And we—" he raised his hand, talon-fingered and pale as bone— "we will claim it. The child will be ours."

The Hunt Begins

The vampires moved as one, their unity forged not of loyalty but of hunger. Orders spread like shadow, silent and swift. The weakest were sent as fodder, the strongest as hunters, and the cleverest as spies.

They did not march. They did not gallop. They drifted from the cathedral like a tide of living shadow; a murder of predators loosed upon the forest.

Above them, the beacon blazed brighter, drawing them onward.

The Geomancers thought they were baiting wolves. But the wolves were not the only beasts circling the trap.

And Count Arad, on his throne of bone, whispered to the night with the confidence of centuries:

"Let them think they hold the fire. It will be we who walk away from the ashes."

Lord Elden

The forest did not hear them. The leaves did not stir at their passage. The earth itself seemed to hold its breath as the hunting party glided through the night. A dozen vampires, lean and ravenous, moved in perfect silence, their forms a blur of shadow and silver teeth. They were not men. They were not wolves. They were death given flesh.

At their head was Lord Elden Ferrow, his amber eyes gleaming like twin lanterns in the dark. He was beautiful in a way that unnerved mortals—his sharp cheekbones, his dark hair, his smile that promised pleasure even as it concealed fangs. But beneath that beauty lay a hunger, a cruelty sharpened by centuries. He had once been a man of the alehouse, fearless and reckless, slipping from tavern to tavern by moonlight. A man who laughed at whispers of disappearances even as he slipped through windows, bold and charming. It had been in the shadows outside a married woman's home, in the thrill of a forbidden tryst, that fate had found him. One bite had stolen his mortal heart, and his first act as a vampire had been to drag the woman he sought into darkness and drink her dry.

From that night, Elden had never looked back. Charm, wit, and a ruthless mind had carried him swiftly to power. He was no brute; he was a predator who studied every flaw, every hesitation, and struck where it would matter most. Now, he was Count Arad's chosen hound, unleashed to claim a prize greater than any kingdom—Faustus, the wolf-child bound in Geomancy.

The Hunt

The beacon was their guide, a thrumming, radiant pulse of power that pulled at their senses with every step. It was not subtle; it was not hidden. It screamed through the night like blood pouring into a starving mouth.

The hunting party flowed over the old bones of human kingdoms: collapsed walls draped in ivy, villages swallowed by weeds, towers broken and hollow. Where once bells had tolled and children had laughed, only silence remained. The ruins paid silent homage to the predators who now ruled the dark.

They crossed through werewolf-marked territory—trees clawed with warnings, the air sharp with musk and rage. One of Elden's lieutenants sniffed the air, lips curling. "Shall we scatter them, lord? Take a trophy?"

Elden silenced him with a glance and a cruel half-smile. "No. Dogs bark at passing shadows. Let them. Our prey is sweeter."

The Scent of Rivals

Then it came—new on the wind. A scent both strange and familiar: wolf and human, Geomancy and desperation braided together. Elden froze, nostrils flaring, eyes narrowing. Slowly, the smile returned to his lips, sharper this time.

"They are not alone in their foolish race," he murmured. "A mother. A broken alpha. And another of the blood. Desperate, running toward the same beacon as we." His voice dropped to a whisper that chilled the hunting party. "Perfect."

The vampires shifted eagerly, their fangs glinting.

"They will lead us to the child," Elden continued. "Let them bleed, let them struggle, let them believe themselves clever. While they stumble through traps and blades, we will wait at the end. They will fall into the jaws of the Geomancers' snare, and in the chaos..." His eyes flashed like gold in firelight. "...we will take the prize. Remember: the boy is not to be slain. He is to be claimed. Only if capture is impossible do we drink him."

The order was not shouted but whispered, a hiss of iron that every vampire obeyed.

The Silent Advance

The hunting party surged forward, their pace relentless. They did not leap or crash through the forest like wolves. They slid between trees, melting into fog, their eyes fixed on the distant silhouette of the Sanctum. Its wards glimmered faintly in the horizon, like a cage waiting to spring shut.

But Elden was not fooled. He knew the Geomancers thought themselves clever, laying bait with one hand and holding fire in the other. He welcomed it. He thrived on turning traps into opportunities.

As the forest swallowed them once more, his voice lingered in the night:

"They think themselves hunters. But we are the true predators. The Sanctum has opened its gates... and we are already inside."

Interlude: Court of Shadows

The cathedral's ruined vaults trembled faintly with the hum of the Geomantic beacon. Count Arad sat high upon his throne of bone, the golden cup of blood wine gleaming faintly in his pale hand. His eyes glowed like molten amber, surveying his court with the detached patience of one who had watched centuries grind kingdoms to dust.

Below him stood two of his most trusted lieutenants—Lord Elden Ferrow, handsome, poised, every inch the predator-commander, and **Rosianna Holt**, older, sharper, her black pearl eyes hardened by centuries of bitter service.

"The Sanctum bleeds its power into the world," Arad murmured, his voice carrying like silk over broken glass. "And we will claim the source."

He turned his gaze on Elden. "You will lead the hunt. Capture the wolf-child, and do not waste him. If the Geomancers have birthed a weapon, then that weapon shall be ours."

Elden bowed, graceful as a dancer. "It will be done, my lord."

The court murmured approval. All but Rosianna.

Her jaw tightened, her nails biting into her palms. She had been with Arad since the first nights, since she tore her own children from their beds in her hunger. She had burned her humanity to ash to earn her place. And yet this... this charming upstart, once a tavern rogue, was given the honor of seizing destiny itself.

"My lord," Rosianna said at last, her voice smooth, but carrying an edge sharp as a blade. "It is curious. Some of us have stood at your side for centuries, carved our loyalty into the very stones of this hall. And yet it is the youngest who is sent to cradle the fate of our kind. Do you fear your elders cannot finish the task?"

The court fell into silence.

Arad did not frown. He did not scold. He smiled, slow and thin, and his gaze cut between them like a knife. "Loyalty is the stone upon which this throne is built," he said softly. "But hunger... hunger is the flame that keeps it alive. Elden is hungry. Ambition still burns in him. You, Rosianna, have the wisdom of age, the patience of the cold. Do you not see? I keep you both. A throne cannot stand on stone alone. Nor can it burn without fire."

His eyes lingered on her, amber and merciless. "Do not mistake envy for wisdom, my child. Watch Elden. Learn from him. And when the time is right, perhaps you will seize what he claims."

Rosianna bowed, but her eyes did not leave Elden's. Cold, sharp, and burning with a promise.

Elden caught her gaze and offered a faint, mocking smile, as though savoring her silent fury.

Count Arad drank deeply from his cup. "Go, then. Both of you. The forest waits. The beacon calls. Bring me my prize."

The court broke into murmurs once more. The hunt had begun—but so had a rivalry that could tear the vampire legions apart from within.

CHAPTER TWENTY-THREE

THE
CONVERGENCE

THE STANDOFF

T he vampires moved with a silent, unnatural grace, no living creature able to match their glide across the earth. The forest floor—tangled roots, damp moss, and broken stones—offered no resistance to their predatory rhythm. They were one body, one will, each step drawn forward by the raw pulse of Faustus's power.

At their head, Lord Elden raised a hand, and instantly the hunting party froze. A dozen shadows became statues at the edge of a clearing. Before them lay a scarred battlefield of jagged stones, remnants of some long-forgotten war. The air itself seemed to remember death here.

Across that same clearing, hidden in the opposite tree line, stood Bella, Emor, and Bryn.

The First Scent

Elden's nostrils flared, his eyes narrowing. The scent of wolves was strong—fresh, close—and threaded within it was something more fragile but infinitely more intriguing: humanity. His amber eyes glinted with satisfaction. Not a random prey. Not a meaningless quarry. This was the scent of the boy's bloodline, faint but undeniable.

A cruel smile touched his lips. "The children are playing in our path," he murmured, voice like ice caressing steel. "And they carry the key to our prize."

Behind him, Rosianna Holt's dark pearl eyes lingered on Elden, envy flickering beneath her obedient bow. She said nothing, but her silence was edged like a blade.

The Warning in Stone

Bella felt them first. It wasn't scent, nor sound. It was the absence of life—the unnatural void vampires carried wherever they moved. Her breath caught, her body seizing in terror. She seized Emor's arm, her nails digging into his weathered skin, and mouthed a silent warning.

Emor's face darkened, his earth-brown eyes sharpening into predator's steel. He lifted his staff slightly, the carved wood humming with the weight of his power. Bryn, already tense, crouched lower, his hazel eyes scanning the gloom, his muscles drawn taut as bowstrings.

"They're here," Bella whispered. "Not humans... not wolves. Something colder."

A Fragile Standoff

The two parties now faced one another across a hundred yards of broken, haunted earth.

The vampires, a dozen hunters led by Elden, eyes burning with hunger and confidence.

The wolves, only two and a woman, desperate, fragile, and out-matched.

And behind all of them, the Sanctum, waiting, patient, its beacon pulsing like a war drum.

The clearing was no mere ground—it was a stage, and the first act of a bloody convergence had begun.

Elden's Command

Elden raised his voice, though still soft enough that it slithered through the air rather than broke it.

"Do not kill them," he ordered, his tone a silken promise of cruelty. His gaze fixed on Bella; her human scent braided with the unmistakable resonance of Faustus. "Take the woman alive. The others... are inconsequential."

The vampires' amber eyes glowed in agreement. The werewolves stiffened. Bella's heart hammered in her chest, but she did not look away.

Three Factions, One Doom

Above them all, Faustus's beacon pulsed—raw, untamed, unrelenting. A heartbeat of power that drew predator and protector alike.

The vampires saw a prize, a weapon to claim.

The werewolves saw a son, a bloodline to protect.

The Geomancers saw a trap, already sprung, their apocalypse baited and waiting.

The broken stones of the battlefield held its breath. The convergence had come.

CHAPTER TWENTY-FOUR

THE BLOOD AND THE MOON

THE TRAITOR

T he silence broke like glass.

"Now," Lord Elden commanded, his voice a whisper sharpened into a blade.

The vampires launched themselves forward, their bodies a blur of darkness and hunger. They struck with impossible speed, claws and fangs gleaming in the silver light of the moon. The clearing erupted into chaos—cold, feral grace against desperate, primal defiance.

Emor roared, his old lungs summoning the power of a warrior who had never bowed, not to man nor beast. His ironwood staff swung wide, cracking against the skull of the first vampire to cross the stones. Bryn shifted mid-leap, his form a violent fusion of man and wolf, claws extended, his hazel eyes burning with fury.

The battle was bloody, immediate, inevitable.

The Betrayal

The night air stank of iron and fear. The clearing, jagged with old stone, became an arena where fates collided. Emor raised his ironwood staff, Bryn crouched low with claws bared, and Bella's heart pounded like a trapped bird.

Then the betrayal struck.

A shadow slipped behind Emor—not vampire, but wolf. Vlad Karlov. Once a loyal brother-in-arms, now a knife in the dark. His claws tore into Emor's back, deep and merciless. The old alpha staggered, his roar twisting into a broken gasp.

"Father!" Bryn's cry was half howl, half human agony.

Blood spilled hot onto the cold earth. Emor fell to his knees, eyes wide not with fear, but with sorrow. He had lived too long to fear death—but not long enough to shield his son from betrayal.

Vlad's grin gleamed, cold as moonlight. "The old ways die tonight." He shoved Emor to the ground and slipped into the vampire ranks, accepted without question.

Bryn's howl tore through the night, a sound of rage so raw that the stones themselves seemed to tremble. He lunged at the vampires, his grief a weapon, his body a storm. Claws tore, fangs snapped—two vampires fell under his fury—but there were too many.

Bella froze, her Geomancy drowned in the psychic storm of Faustus's beacon. She could only watch as father fell, son raged, and traitor vanished.

The night was broken. And the worst was yet to come.

The Fall of Emor

Emor's roar broke, twisting into a guttural gasp of shock and pain. His body staggered under the sudden betrayal, knees buckling, staff falling from his hands. His mouth spilled crimson, and the fire in his eyes dimmed as life bled out of him.

"Father!" Bryn's howl shattered the clearing, a scream of rage and grief that split the night like thunder.

Emor, the broken alpha, the grieving father, was gone before he touched the ground. His body crumpled in the blood-soaked stones, his spirit silenced by his own kin.

Bryn's grief fueled his rage, but rage blinded him. He hurled himself at Vlad with reckless fury, his claws desperate for vengeance. But the vampires, quick to seize the moment, slipped past him.

The clearing became a funnel.

Emor was gone.

Bryn was trapped in a duel of betrayal.

And Bella—Bella stood alone, exposed, a fragile figure of glowing hands and frantic Geomancy.

Lord Elden, his amber eyes locked on her, advanced with measured precision. Each step was a hunter's promise. Bella's magic flared, half-formed spells sparking in her trembling hands, but she could feel the weight of inevitability pressing down on her.

She was no longer a fighter. She was prey.

The Traitor's Reward

Vlad stepped back from Bryn; his bloody claws lifted not in shame but in triumph. His face was calm, almost serene, as though the act of patricide had finally cleansed him of the shadow he had always lived in.

He turned to the vampire line, his path clear, his allegiance chosen.

Lord Elden's gaze slid to him, and with the faintest nod of approval, the traitor was welcomed. Vlad Karlov had paid his price in blood, and his reward was a promise whispered in silence.

The clearing, lit by the cruel silver light of the moon, had become a stage of betrayal, blood, and looming conquest. Bella's breath caught in her chest as Elden closed the distance. The trap was sprung, the prize within his grasp.

The Blood and the Moon had chosen its victims.

Bella's Capture

The world spun in silver and crimson. Emor's body lay still upon the stones, his lifeblood soaking into the earth, and Bryn's howls of grief shattered the clearing. But Bella had no time for mourning—her enemy was already upon her.

Lord Elden closed the distance with a predator's patience, each step measured, each movement inevitable. His hunting party fanned out in a half-circle, cutting off every escape. Bella's hands glowed with desperate light, her Geomancy sparking raw and unstable, but she could feel her own panic unraveling the spell before it was born.

She thrust her palms forward. The ground trembled, roots snapping like whips from the soil. For an instant, the air crackled with promise. A wall of jagged earth rose between her and Elden.

But he only laughed.

With inhuman speed, he leapt, his body a blur. The barrier crumbled beneath his claws as if it were dust. He landed before her, towering, his amber eyes gleaming with cold satisfaction.

Bella stumbled backward, clutching at the glow in her hands. "Stay back!" she cried, though her voice trembled.

"You are no hunter," Elden said softly. "You are bait. And now—my prize."

The Fall

Bryn, locked in furious combat with Vlad, saw too late what was happening. His claws tore across the traitor's chest, but Vlad only laughed, blood pouring yet body unbroken, buying the vampires precious seconds.

"Bella!" Bryn roared, but his voice was drowned in the clash of fangs and steel.

Bella tried again, weaving a desperate spell, but Elden's hand shot out, faster than sight. His grip closed around her throat, lifting her from the ground as though she were nothing more than a child's doll. Her legs kicked, her hands clawed at his iron grasp, but the air refused to fill her lungs. The glow of her Geomancy flickered, dimmed, then guttered out.

She managed only a rasp of protest, a whisper meant for her son: "Faustus..."

Elden's smile widened. "Yes. Through you, we will have him."

The Capture Sealed

The vampires closed ranks around their lord, shielding him as he held Bella aloft. One produced chain of dark iron, each link etched with runes that drank the faint glow of her Geomancy. They wrapped her wrists, her throat, her ankles. The moment the final clasp clicked shut, her power was silenced.

She sagged in Elden's grip, half-conscious, eyes wide with grief and terror.

Bryn broke free from Vlad's assault, his body streaked with blood and fury. He lunged, but Elden was already retreating, his hunters flowing back into the night with their captive.

"Bella!" Bryn's cry split the clearing, but the only answer was the echo of the vampires' retreat, swift and merciless.

Vlad staggered, laughing through the blood pouring from his wounds. "She is theirs now. And soon—the boy will be too."

Bryn's eyes burned with vengeance, but inside him, sorrow threatened to consume all reason.

The Moon's Witness

Above, the moon watched in silence, its pale light a cruel witness to betrayal, capture, and despair. The blood of wolves stained the stones. The scent of vampires lingered like poison.

And in the distance, within the Sanctum's walls, Faustus stirred—his mother's agony echoing through the bond that tied them still.

The blood had been spilled. The moon had claimed its due. And the game had changed forever.

CHAPTER TWENTY-FIVE

CHAINS AND ECHOS

IN THE VAMPIRE'S GRASP

The world narrowed to the clinking of rune-etched chains and the iron scent of her own fear. Bella was dragged through the ruins of an old city, its spires broken like teeth, until she was thrown to her knees in the cathedral of Count Arad DeLavoit.

The throne of carved bone loomed before her. Arad, ageless and regal, swirled blood-wine in a golden chalice, his amber eyes never leaving her face. Elden stood proudly beside him, one hand still smeared with her blood, a hunter displaying his prize.

"Bella," Arad said, his voice like velvet drawn over steel. "The wolf's whore. The Geomancer's traitor. And yet... the mother of the anomaly." He leaned forward, hunger and curiosity warring in his gaze. "Tell me of the boy. Tell me of his fire."

Bella's lips tightened. She said nothing.

From the shadows, Rosianna Holt emerged, her black-pearl eyes narrowed. She circled Bella with slow, deliberate steps, her envy sharpening each word.

"You give Elden glory, woman," she whispered, her fangs flashing. "But you are nothing. A chain, a weakness. Do you think your silence protects your son? You will watch him fall, and your suffering will be our feast."

Bella's heart clenched. But she only whispered to herself: *Hold on, Faustus. Hold on.*

Faustus, the Lunar Agony

Far away, within the Sanctum's cold stone halls, Faustus bolted upright in his chamber. His chains rattled as his body convulsed. His heart slammed against his ribs.

He could feel it. Her fear. Her pain.

"Mother..." The word was raw, torn from his throat.

The Heartstones around him shuddered, their crimson glow flickering wildly. Lycah burst into the chamber, her chants already rising, but Faustus's eyes blazed with light brighter than any sigil. The tether snapped like brittle twine.

The moon's call surged through him. His hands warped into claws, his breath became a growl, and with a scream that shook the very Sanctum, he shattered his restraints.

Bella, the Court's Cruelty

The vampires pressed closer, feeding on her terror like wolves circling wounded prey. Elden knelt beside her, his smile cruel. "He feels you, doesn't he? That bond cannot be severed. He will come to us. You will bring him."

Bella spat blood at his boots. "He will come—but not for you."

Elden's hand struck her face, sharp and cold. But before he could deliver another blow, Arad raised a single finger. Silence fell like a shroud.

"No," the Count said softly. "She is precious. Not to be broken. Not yet. She will be the chain around the beast's neck. And through her, we will own him."

Rosianna's lips curled in bitter envy, her gaze flicking between Bella and Elden.

Faustus, the Breaking Storm

Back in the Sanctum, Faustus's roar cracked stone from the ceiling. The elders scrambled to reinforce the wards, but Lycah staggered back, terror dawning in her eyes.

"He has heard her," she whispered. "The mother's voice. The bond is stronger than the tether."

Faustus's gaze burned like the moon itself. His voice, deeper, half-human, half-wolf, rolled like thunder:

"I will find you. I will tear them apart."

The Sanctum trembled with his vow.

CHAPTER TWENTY-SIX

THE CUT

VAMPIRE LAIR

The vampire lair was no cathedral of splendor but a tomb of forgotten hope. Beneath the ruins of a once-grand church, cold stone pressed in on all sides. Chains rattled faintly in the damp, stagnant air, and the walls wept with centuries of decay. Here, the sun had never touched, and only whispers of dread remained.

Bella was dragged into the deepest chamber, her wrists bound in iron that bit into her skin, her Geomancy silent—a dead weight crushed beneath fear and exhaustion. The glow of torchlight revealed jagged carvings along the walls, old runes whose meanings had long since rotted into superstition.

Lord Elden stood above her like an executioner poised over the block. His face, carved with cruel perfection, betrayed no warmth, only an ageless cruelty that made the dungeon seem colder still.

"The child," he said, his voice as sharp as ice breaking across a frozen lake. "Tell me of him. Tell me of his powers. Tell me how the Geomancers wrought such a thing. Tell me everything."

Bella's body ached, her cheek raw from the blow of capture, but her spirit burned stubbornly. She lifted her chin. "I will tell you nothing." Her voice, though cracked and weary, held a core of iron.

Elden's laugh was soft, hollow, and humorless. It echoed across the stone like a blade scraped against bone. "Brave little human," he murmured. "But bravery is a luxury you will not afford for long. You are not merely a prisoner—you are the bridge. The key. The psychic tether to the storm we seek. And if words fail me, I will carve truth from your bones."

The vampire lair was not a cavern of gothic splendor, but a dungeon of cold stone and iron, buried deep beneath the cathedral's ruins. Damp air clung to the walls, and the silence of centuries hung like a shroud. Bella was dragged through winding passages, her wrists bound in chains, her Geomancy a useless weight in her skull. The darkness pressed in on her, alive with the whispers of things long buried.

At the heart of the dungeon, Lord Elden waited. His figure was a monolith of control, tall and poised, his eyes twin embers of polished amber. He studied her as one might study a rare and dangerous relic.

"The child," he said, his voice a smooth blade, sharp and cold. "Tell me of its powers. Tell me how the Geomancers shaped it. Tell me everything."

Bruised, bloodied, but unbroken, Bella raised her chin. Her voice was hoarse, but steady. "I will tell you nothing."

Elden's lips curved into something that was not a smile but a mockery of one. "Brave," he said, his tone almost indulgent. "But bravery is a fleeting thing. You are not a warrior. You are a bridge. A psychic link to the boy. We do not need your words—we only need to break you."

He gestured, and Griseld Pitt stepped forward. Her face, pale as porcelain, was beautiful in a cruel, doll-like way. Her eyes, black pearls filled with malice, gleamed as her long, sharpened claw unfurled. She moved with unnatural grace, closing the distance to Bella in an instant.

The strike was meant to disfigure, not kill. But Bella, with one last, desperate plea to the earth, tore a shard of stone from the dungeon floor. It erupted upward, forcing Griseld's hand off course. The claw slashed from temple to jaw, leaving a jagged scar but sparing Bella's eye.

Bella screamed, the pain white-hot and blinding. Griseld hissed in frustration, drawing back, eager to strike again. But Elden's hand shot out, halting her.

"That is enough," he commanded. His tone was calm, but the force behind it was absolute. Griseld froze, her chest rising and falling with fury she dared not release.

Elden crouched before Bella. He reached out, his fingers tracing the fresh wound. He lifted them to his lips, tasting the blood. His eyes flickered—something sharp, something distant. "This blood... it is unlike any I have known. A taste of something... older." His voice dropped to a murmur, more to himself than to her. "The scent of roses. The ashes of fire. A lullaby in the dark."

For an instant, Bella felt the world tilt. She did not know the lullaby he whispered of, nor why the smell of roses suddenly haunted her memory. But her heart lurched, as though a phantom hand had reached from the past and gripped her.

Elden's gaze lingered on her, intent, unnerving. "A scar is but skin. The true wound will come when your child screams for you—and you cannot answer."

Behind him, Griseld's jaw clenched. She lowered her claw, but her eyes narrowed, lingering not on Bella, but on Elden. For the first time in centuries, she saw his attention fixed not on the throne, nor the court, nor even conquest—but on a fragile, bloodied human. Something ugly and dangerous stirred in her, though she kept her silence.

Bella, her face wet with blood and tears, knew only this: she was alive, but she was no longer free. She was not to be killed, nor turned, but kept. A tool. A tether. And the scar carved into her flesh was only the beginning of the torment that awaited her.

CHAPTER TWENTY-SEVEN

THE LONE WOLF'S VOW

VENGEANCE

The clearing was death-silent, the air thick with the bitter tang of blood and fine black dust. It was a graveyard of failure, and Bryn stood in the middle of it like a shadow carved from grief.

Emor's body lay still before him, the ironwood staff at his side. Once, his father had been a storm and a mountain, a warrior whose presence bent the will of others like trees before the wind. Now he was only stone and silence, a broken vessel returning to the earth.

Bryn dropped to his knees, his claws sinking into the soil. His chest heaved, and for the first time in years, his hands trembled. He reached out and brushed the old wolf's face, cold beneath his palm. A single tear slid down his cheek — not weakness, but the raw, uncontainable truth of loss. It cut deeper than any fang or claw could.

He dug the grave with his bare hands. Every thrust into the earth was a curse, every handful of dirt a bitter prayer. When the shallow pit was finished, he lowered Emor into it, his jaw clenched against a sob that threatened to tear free. "Father," he rasped, his voice little more than gravel, "I swear this won't be the end. I'll make them pay."

But as he rose, another image burned into his mind: Bella's wide, desperate eyes. Her trembling hands. Her stubborn hope that had dragged them all down this path. Rage boiled through him. If she had stayed hidden, if she had heeded Emor's warnings, his father would still live. Vlad would never have found his moment. This ruin was hers.

And yet—his chest tightened as another memory struck. Not of her failure, but of her fire. The way she had stood unarmed against Terrek, her voice steady when wolves twice her size threatened her. The way her gaze held the same defiance that Orin once carried. For a heartbeat, he saw Orin in her. Saw the same strange kindness that had always unsettled him. It hurt worse than the grief.

Bryn shook the thought away, growling low. Kindness was weakness. And yet, hadn't it been Orin's kindness that made him stronger than them all?

His oath solidified, a vow carved in blood and stone. He would hunt the vampires who had taken Bella. He would tear Vlad apart for his betrayal. And when he found Faustus — Orin's boy, the last thread of his bloodline — he would protect him, no matter the cost. Not for Bella. Never for her. For Orin. For blood.

Still, beneath the vow's iron edge, something darker and more complicated coiled: the truth that he could not separate his oath to the boy from the woman who bore him. Even in his hatred, he was bound to her.

Bryn tilted back his head and howled. It was not the cry of a pack — there was no pack left. It was the promise of a lone wolf. A vow of vengeance, a cry that made the forest scatter in fear. It was not a call for kin. It was the herald of a hunt that would not end until the earth itself drank his enemies' blood.

The lone wolf had been born in sorrow. Now he would live in vengeance.

The Hunt Begins

The lone wolf slipped through the forest, his body low and silent, a predator honed by loss. Every step was measured, every breath a calculation. The trees blurred around him, their branches whispering in the cold night wind, but his senses were razor-sharp, tuned to the faintest trace of his quarry.

The air carried the copper sting of vampire breath, the cloying perfume of blood turned sour. Beneath it, sharper still, was the musk of a wolf gone rotten — Vlad. The scent of betrayal curled Bryn's lips into a snarl. His stomach turned at the memory of claws driven into Emor's back, of crimson pouring from a father's mouth. The hatred was visceral, all-consuming.

Yet beneath those trails, faint as smoke after a fire, lingered another scent: Bella's. It was fragile, laced with fear and desperation, but stubbornly alive. Bryn froze, his chest tightening. For a moment, instinct surged — the fierce, protective impulse to find her, to shield her, to tear apart anything that dared to touch her. Then reason struck like ice. He growled low in his throat. *She is the reason we are here. She is the reason he is dead.*

Still... he could not banish the echo of Orin in her face, in her defiance. He hated her, yet he could not let her go. Not while Faustus lived.

He wove through the undergrowth, avoiding the open ground, his every movement the rhythm of a seasoned hunter. The beacon of Faustus's power thrummed louder in his skull, a constant, chaotic vibration that grew more violent the nearer he drew to the Sanctum. It was not hope. It was not a call. It was the ticking of a war-drum, promising ruin.

Bryn's claws flexed as he ran. His vow was etched into his bones: the vampires would pay, Vlad would die screaming, and Bella — curse her name, curse her choices — would be dragged back from the dark even if it cost him the last shred of his soul. Not for her. Never for her. For Orin. For Faustus.

But in the back of his mind, quieter than a breath, an unspoken truth gnawed at him. The vow was no longer just for the dead. It was also for the living woman he both despised and could not abandon.

The lone wolf ran faster, his fury and his grief a fire in his veins. Ahead, the vampires closed in. Beyond them, the Sanctum pulsed with power, a storm waiting to break. The hunt had begun.

CHAPTER TWENTY-EIGHT

THE AWAKENING OF THE STORM

A MOTHER'S PAIN

Inside the Sanctum, the chamber was a cold monument of stone and ritual. But within Faustus's mind, the storm had begun.

The hum had always been there — a faint, psychic vibration at the back of his skull, the tether that bound him to Magistra Lycah's will. But now, with every pulse of his mother's pain echoing through him, the hum frayed. It was no longer constant; it flickered, weakened, and cracked like a rope under strain.

The visions came first. His mother's cheek stung as if it were his own, the cold vampire hand pressed to her skin burned in his bones. A child's heart, unprepared for such torment, filled with a rage so sharp it made his vision blur. His power stirred — not in explosions, but in ripples. The stones beneath his feet shivered. Hairline cracks spread like veins across the floor. A faint wind whispered where no air should move.

He was afraid. The memories he had never known pressed at him — a lullaby half-remembered, a warmth that had once been his, a mother's face blurred by time. They sharpened the agony but also gave it meaning. The tether frayed further.

The Geomancers had miscalculated. They had thought pain would shape him. But Faustus was learning pain could also sharpen him. Not yet free, not yet unbound, but dangerous — because for the first time, the storm within him had direction.

The Scent of a Geomancer

Bryn crested the final ridge of the old mountain pass, his breath a mist of fury in the night. Below him, bathed in pale moonlight, sprawled the Geomancers' Sanctum. Once a fortress of impenetrable wards and cold precision, it now shimmered like a wounded beast. The protective barrier, once a seamless wall of invisible energy, flickered erratically, collapsing and reforming like the dying pulse of a star.

The air vibrated with a discordant hum, the psychic scream of Faustus's untamed power bleeding through every stone. The rocks trembled beneath Bryn's feet, the mountain itself groaning under the strain of magic torn from its foundations. The Sanctum was unraveling—not by siege, but from within.

Below, in the moon-washed field, shadows moved in disciplined formation. Vampires. An army of them. Bryn's eyes locked on the regal figure at their head: Lord Elden, calm and merciless, his stride unhurried. And beside him, the traitor—Vlad—his wolf-stench reeking even at this distance, his hands forever marked by Emor's blood. Bryn's claws dug into the earth.

He understood then that the Sanctum was no fortress but a lure. The Geomancers had torn open their walls, dangling Faustus like bait. The vampires, drunk on the scent of power, were marching straight into the trap.

But Bryn was not here for politics, nor vengeance alone. His nose, keener than sight, caught the faint, cold scent threading through the chaos—the tether. Not Faustus's raw storm, but the clinical aroma of the one holding him back. Elixirs. Parchment. The scent of a Geomancer. He followed it with a hunter's certainty: the central spire.

Moving low, Bryn slipped into the fractured wards, the gaps wide enough to swallow him whole. The Sanctum's bones shuddered as he crossed its threshold. He no longer cared for armies or traps. He was stalking the one chain keeping his nephew bound.

And in the tower, amid runes that glowed cold and crystalline, he found her.

Magistra Lycah.

She stood before a towering Heartstone, her hands ablaze with icy light, her gaze fixed on the storm she believed she controlled. When she turned at his entrance, there was no fear—only fanatic conviction.

"You are too late," she whispered. "The ritual is in motion. The boy is ours. The world will be remade."

Bryn's lips peeled back in a snarl. Words meant nothing. He launched himself forward—fang, claw, and unrelenting grief made flesh. Crystals shattered in showers of dust. Wards screamed and broke. His strike was merciless, his claws tearing through her throat.

Her death cry was swallowed by the storm. And as her body collapsed, the tether she held snapped. Not gently. Violently.

The Sanctum wailed as if the earth itself had been wounded.

CHAPTER TWENTY-NINE

THE BREAKING OF THE CHAINS

BELLA'S WRATH

F ar below, in the damp dungeon of the vampire lair, Bella staggered as the psychic snap ripped through her. For a heartbeat, she felt nothing—then everything.

The tether was gone.

A shockwave of pure, untamed energy tore outward, rattling stone, shattering chains. It wasn't just Geomancy. It was Faustus—his rage, his love, his desperate, wordless cry for her.

Iron links glowed white-hot before clattering to the floor, useless. Bella's cheek, still marked with the scar Griseld had left, burned as though lit from within. The energy flooding her was both alien and familiar—a reminder of the terrible truth Myr had whispered when she was a child.

Her power, dormant for so long, surged awake.

Lord Elden, caught in the blast, staggered against the wall, his predatory calm torn to tatters. For the first time in centuries, true fear flickered in his amber eyes. Griseld shrieked, clutching her skull as Bella's power slammed her into stone.

Bella turned, her voice low and furious. "You touched me. You hurt him. For that, I should let the sun feast on you."

Light seared from her fingertips, cutting across Elden's cheek. He screamed, clutching at the wound, dark ichor streaming between his fingers. His retreat was a blur, his escape a shadow fleeing her wrath. Whether he survived or not, Bella did not linger to see.

She pressed her palm against the dungeon wall. Stone groaned and shifted beneath her command, opening a path to freedom. Her voice was steady, dangerous.

"I'm coming, Faustus."

The Unbound

The moment the psychic tether snapped, a profound silence fell across Bella's mind. The chaotic, discordant scream of her son's power was gone, replaced by a resonant hum — deep, terrifying, and beautiful. For the first time, the world did not overwhelm her; it bent to her will with crystalline clarity.

The dungeon itself responded. The ancient stone walls groaned, the veins of earth pulsed like living arteries, and the iron chains binding her glowed white-hot before snapping, links clattering to the floor in a rain of sparks.

Lord Elden staggered back, amber eyes wide, his predator's mask cracking into something colder: fear. For centuries, he had been the hunter.

Now, in Bella, he saw something else — not a trembling prisoner, but a storm given flesh.

Griseld shrieked, still clutching her head from the psychic blast. Before she could recover, the dungeon floor heaved. A violent surge of Geomantic energy struck her like a hammer, hurling her against the wall. Stone cracked, dust rained down, and she collapsed in a broken heap.

Elden tried to gather himself, but Bella turned toward him with terrifying calm. Her voice was no longer that of a desperate mother but of a judge pronouncing sentence.

"You dared put your hands on me," she hissed. "I will hang you by your feet and lay you out for the sun to devour."

Her hands glowed with searing light, and she cast her first true spell. A razor-edged blade of brilliance slashed across Elden's face. He screamed, clutching his cheek as a deep gash spilled dark, burgundy blood.

The walls trembled with her fury, and for a moment, it seemed she might end him where he stood. But Elden, even wounded, was no fool. In a blur of shadow and rage, he retreated, vanishing into the collapsing corridors. His scream echoed, then faded, leaving only silence and dust. Whether he lived or perished in the ruin was unclear.

Bella stood alone, her breath ragged, her face a mask of fury and resolve. The wound Griseld had given her now glowed faintly blue, the scar sealing but refusing to vanish. It was a mark of what had been done to her — and what she had become.

At her feet, one of Elden's lesser vampires still writhed, too slow to escape. She raised a hand, and the floor rippled like liquid beneath him, swallowing his body in molten stone. His final scream was cut short as the earth closed over him, leaving no trace.

The dungeon was silent again. Bella pressed her hands to the wall, and the earth itself answered. Rock shifted, crumbled, and yielded to her command. A tunnel began to open — a path upward, a path to her son.

She was no longer a prisoner, no longer a fugitive. She was the unbound, and the world would learn to fear her.

CHAPTER THIRTY

THE ECHO OF SILENCE

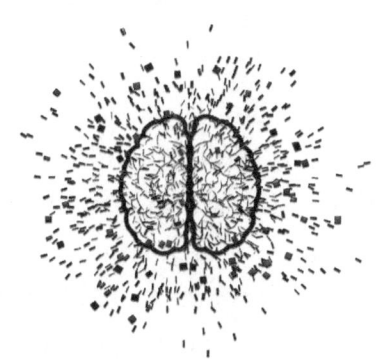

THE COLLAPSE

There had always been a hum. Cold. Unyielding. The very fabric of Faustus's prison. It was not sound, but command. It was silence masquerading as control.

And then, one moment — it was gone.

The silence that followed was not peace. It was deafening. The world poured into him all at once: the low groan of the earth, the threads of moonlight pulling through the stones, the restless pulse of life in every root and river vein. It was too much, too vast. His mind reeled, but it did not collapse. Instead, it adjusted.

Every breath of air was laced with energy. Every step he took set faint ripples across the broken runes, like water disturbed by a falling leaf. The Sanctum itself seemed to watch him now, its walls no longer holding him, but trembling at his presence.

The boy was still there — frightened, disoriented — but the Lunar Geomancer within him pressed close, like a second shadow. It was not yet unleashed, only coiled, patient, waiting. And for the first time, Faustus realized the chain that had held it was gone.

The silence was not absence. It was freedom. And it terrified him.

The Visitor

The door to Faustus's cell, a massive ironwood slab studded with runes, tore itself apart in a storm of splinters and warped metal. He did not cause it. The power—an instinctive, hungering thing within him—did. It was an act of raw, unfiltered Lunar Geomancy, a surge so primal and violent that the stones themselves quivered in answer.

A figure entered the chamber, a dark, hulking shape framed in the ruin of the doorway.

Faustus's breath caught. *I have seen this shape before... in dreams.* But the storm inside him surged to the front. He did not know the man—only the threat.

The Lunar Geomancer within him responded with predatory fury. A wave of kinetic force burst outward, slamming the intruder into the far wall. Bone crunched; the figure collapsed in a heap. Faustus felt no pity, only the sharp, detached satisfaction of power unbound.

The man stirred, dragging himself upright with a growl. His voice was hoarse, ragged.
"I know who you are," he whispered.

The words meant nothing. To the storm, they were a distraction, a useless hum. Energy shimmered around Faustus's body, coalescing into a second blow that would finish the intruder—tear him apart like the door before him.

But then—faint, cutting through the roar of the storm—came something else.

A sound, impossibly soft: the ghost of a lullaby.
Not words. Just cadence. A low, tender rhythm he had never been taught, yet recognized as if it were written into his blood.

And with it, a fragrance, delicate and out of place in the damp chamber: the scent of a rose, ashes and bloom entwined.

The storm inside him faltered. The energy around him wavered, a tide pulling back. Faustus froze, his hand trembling mid-air. *What is this?*

The intruder did not speak again. He only watched, sensing the sudden change but unable to grasp its cause.

Faustus's heart pounded. His mind was torn between two worlds: the storm of destruction that begged release, and the lullaby that whispered of something else—warmth, safety, a memory he had never lived but somehow knew.

The scent faded. The song slipped back into silence. The storm surged again, demanding his will.

But for the first time, Faustus hesitated.

Elsewhere in the Sanctum

High in a separate tower, Elder Myr stirred. His senses, always attuned to the psychic tremors of the boy, felt something different ripple through the Sanctum: not chaos, not storm, but resonance. A note of warmth hidden in the cacophony.

He froze.
The lullaby. The rose.

A memory rose unbidden: a child—Bella, small and trembling—once humming the same melody in a moment of fright. And before her, a woman, Bella's mother, whose kindness had been both her greatest strength and the very reason Myr had despised her.

Now the song was here, inside the storm of Faustus.

Myr's expression darkened.

"So," he whispered to himself, "the bloodline endures. The curse of kindness still lingers."

And though he felt a chill of unease, another thought twisted in his mind like a knife:

If I cannot extinguish it... I will use it.

CHAPTER THIRTY-ONE

THE MEMORY OF A MOTHER

HOPE

F austus stood at the precipice of fury, power flooding his veins like molten silver. The Lunar Geomancer inside him screamed for release, to tear, to burn, to annihilate. His hand rose, the air trembling around him, ready to crush the intruder before him.

And then—something else.

Not a sound, but a feeling. A memory.

A soft hand, warm as sunlit earth, cool as fresh water, brushed his cheek. It was impossible—no one had ever touched him with gentleness—but he *remembered* it all the same. A hand that carried the fragrance of roses and soil, a hand that stilled his childish tremors in the dark.

"There, there," a voice murmured, not spoken but resonant in his bones. "Don't cry. I cannot be with you in flesh... but I left a part of myself behind, so that when you needed me most, you would know me."

The melody followed, faint and fragile as morning light: a lullaby. Not the sterile hum of wards or the cold cadence of a ritual, but a song woven from love. It rose and fell like breath, simple and human, a balm against the storm inside him.

For the first time, Faustus saw a face—not sharp and cruel like his wardens, but kind. Worried. Loving. The face of a woman he did not know, yet knew with absolute certainty. *Mother.*

The Lunar Geomancer within him faltered. Fury gave way to something stranger, something far more dangerous to its control. Love.

His breath caught. His chest ached. His voice, unused to emotion, cracked with confusion.

"What is happening to me? I feel... sad. And happy. Both."

The storm began to subside. Not broken, but reshaped. The chaotic, discordant roar settled into a steady hum, as if the moon itself had paused to listen. His eyes, once burning with feral light, dimmed into the deep, vulnerable blue of a child's gaze.

Two selves—the boy and the storm—merged. Not enemies now, but one. And their purpose was no longer destruction. It was singular, radiant, unyielding.

Faustus looked at the intruder, though his attention was far beyond him now. The first word he had ever spoken with true meaning slipped from his lips, rough and raw:

"Mother."

His power shifted. No longer a raging tempest, it became a river with direction, a current with will. The Sanctum, his cage, was no longer an end—it was the beginning. Beyond its walls lay a world he had never seen, but already he knew the path.

A beacon shone within him. A light. A promise. A mother.

"I must go to her," he whispered, a new resolve hardening in his voice. "I must find her."

And for the first time, Faustus's fury bent not to chains, not to fear, but to hope.

Path to the Sanctum

The dungeon wall moaned as if alive, ancient stone groaning under the strain of a will far stronger than iron. With a crack like thunder, it yielded—not in ruin, but in obedience. Rock softened, liquefied, and flowed outward in a river of molten stone, carving a path where none had existed. Bella did not cower at the miracle; she commanded it.

The power was no longer a whisper. It roared through her veins like a storm awakened after a lifetime of silence. Once, her magic had been domestic, quiet—charms for hearth and home, gentle spells for healing or protection. But now? Now it was vast, primal, unbound. The earth itself bent to her, carrying her forward as though eager to see its mistress restored.

And beneath it all pulsed the truth she had felt the moment the tether snapped: Faustus. No longer a captive hum muffled by Geomantic chains, but a blazing resonance—wild, focused, alive. She pressed a trembling hand to her scarred cheek, her breath catching with a mixture of awe and terror. *He is free. My son is free.*

Her steps turned into a relentless march, steady as the heartbeat of the earth beneath her feet. She was no longer fleeing shadows—she was drawing them in. The vampires' scent clung to the wind: cold, iron-tinged, cruel. She could almost taste Lord Elden's malice still burning in the air. A grim resolve hardened her heart. *They will not touch him. They will never touch my family again.*

The forest darkened ahead, the trees bending like wary witnesses to her passage. Then—a blur. A rogue werewolf burst from the underbrush, eyes wild, jaws open in a feral snarl. Bella did not scream. She did not falter. Her hands rose instinctively, her will snapping outward in a violent wave. The beast was hurled through the air as though struck by the invisible hand of the earth itself, landing in a broken sprawl.

Breathless, the creature scrabbled backward on clawed hands, its eyes wide with terror. Bella stepped toward it, her voice cold, commanding.

"Leave, beast. Leave before you beg me for death."

The wolf whimpered, its bravado shattered. It stumbled upright, then fled into the woods with desperate speed, vanishing into shadow.

Bella lingered a moment, staring into the dark where he had gone. Then she turned back, her gaze fixed on the horizon where the Sanctum's walls loomed beneath the pale, merciless moon. Her scar burned, her heart pounded, and her son's call drew her onward.

Nothing would stop her now.

Interlude: The Watcher

High above the fractured Sanctum, in a tower veiled by cold wards and ancient silence, Elder Myr watched. His thin fingers traced the rim of a basin filled with blackened water, the ashes of long-dead Heartstones drifting on its surface like pale petals.

The vision shimmered. He saw her — Bella, breaking through the earth with fire in her veins, her scar still fresh, her Geomancy roaring as though it had finally awakened from centuries of slumber. For a moment, he did not see the scarred, grieving woman the world thought her to be. He saw *her mother*. The same spark. The same dangerous kindness.

He whispered into the basin, though none but the ashes could hear:

"So it awakens again. I warned them... her mother was never truly broken. And now the daughter walks the same cursed path."

Myr leaned closer, his eyes gleaming with a fanatic's hunger and a betrayer's sorrow. He remembered a time when he had walked beside Bella's mother, when he had seen the quiet fury of her power cloaked beneath gentleness. He remembered fearing it — and desiring it. Power born of compassion, sharpened by pain. The rarest and deadliest kind of all.

The basin rippled. In its depths, Faustus flickered like a storm barely contained, his raw Lunar Geomancy cracking the walls of the Sanctum itself. Myr smiled thinly.

"Yes, child. Rage, howl, burn. But you are not the only one who carries the storm. She is the true danger. And she does not yet know it."

He drew the wards tighter around the tower, hiding himself even from his fellow elders. They thought him merely a quiet scholar, a relic of the old council. Let them believe. Let them rot in their arrogance.

"When the time comes," he murmured, his voice a low hiss in the candlelight, *"the mother's power will not be hidden. And then... the world will see which side I choose."*

The ashes in the basin glowed faintly, like the petals of a rose catching fire, before sinking back into darkness.

Chapter Thirty-Two

THE EYE OF THE STORM

The Oath

The ritual chamber was unrecognizable. Walls torn. Floors fractured. The dead scattered like broken dolls. In the eye of it all stood Faustus, glowing faintly in the storm, no longer chaos but controlled resonance.

Bryn stood across from him, battered, bloodied, his claws dripping Lycah's death. He did not speak. He only watched.

Faustus's gaze lifted to him, calm, clear, unsettling in its certainty. He had not lashed out at his uncle. He had chosen restraint. In that moment, predator and child, wolf and Geomancer, understood one another.

Bryn thought of Orin—his brother, dead for love. He thought of the oath of blood that bound him now to this boy. Words crowded his throat: *I am your uncle. Your father was my brother.* But he swallowed them back. Now was not the time.

Instead, they stood in silence.

A wolf of vengeance. A child of storm. Two survivors in the ruins of an empire of hubris. Bound not by choice, but by blood and the storm's will.

A Burdened Heart

The ironwood doors of the Sanctum's ritual chamber, already splintered and broken, shuddered under a final pulse of Geomantic power before collapsing inward. From the threshold stepped Bella, her hands glowing faintly, her scar catching the pale light, her eyes blazing with both fury and longing. She froze.

The chamber was wreckage incarnate—walls cracked, runes shattered, the once-mighty council of Geomancers lying lifeless and broken. Bryn stood among them, battered but standing, his body scarred by grief and battle. Yet Bella's eyes did not linger on ruin or on Bryn.

They found him. Faustus. The boy she had lost. The child she had prayed for. The storm she had feared. He stood in the center of the devastation, not merely a prisoner freed but a Lunar Geomancer in full, terrible bloom. Power shimmered around him like moonlight given form. Yet in the same breath, he was just a boy—her boy. Tears welled in Bella's eyes.

"My son..."

The word broke from her like a prayer.

Faustus turned. The storm inside him—the weapon, the Lunar Geomancer—wavered. For a moment the chamber seemed to still. And then the boy's voice, raw and jubilant, tore free of his chest.

"MOTHER!"

The power that had cloaked him folded back, not vanished but subdued, as though bowing before her presence. He ran—swift, graceful, impossible—and flung himself into her arms. Bella embraced him fiercely, cradling him against her heart, tears streaking her scarred face as her hands, blazing with gentle Geomancy, shielded him. For the first time in his life, Faustus was held, not as a weapon, but as a son.

Bryn watched in silence. His heart, burdened with grief, clenched with conflicting truths. He despised Bella for her choices, for the ruin left in their wake. Yet the bond between her and Faustus was undeniable, radiant as moonlight, and he could not deny his vow. Faustus was his brother's son. Blood of his blood. His to protect.

"Faustus," Bryn said, his voice rough, "your father was my brother. You are all I have left."

Faustus looked at him, still clinging to Bella. "I saw you in my dreams," he whispered, "dying here in this place."

Bryn's jaw tightened. "That was not me. It was my twin. Your father."

Faustus said nothing more, only nodded slowly, as if the truth were a stone he placed inside himself to keep safe.

And so, they stood together: a scarred mother whose power now stirred the bones of the earth, a broken wolf who had lost everything but his oath, and a boy reborn as something more than weapon, more than prisoner—something loved.

The storm outside still raged. The moon still loomed above. But within the ruined chamber of the Sanctum, for the first time in years, a family had been made whole.

Chapter Thirty-Three

The Howl of the Pack

Ian Grok

F ar from the crumbling walls of the Sanctum, beneath the pale silver eye of the full moon, a pack of werewolves gathered on a windswept ridge. Their fur bristled, their claws dug into the earth, and their eyes glowed with the wildfire of lunar light. The night was heavy with tension, for the moon was no longer just a distant guide—it had become something alive, something awake, and every wolf in the circle felt it.

Alpha Ian Grok, scarred and massive, lifted his head and inhaled deeply. His black eyes narrowed as the pulse reached him—not a hum, not the Geomancers' leash that had hung like a chain over the earth for years, but a furious, rhythmic roar of unbound power. He rumbled low in his chest, then loosed a thunderous howl that split the night. The sound rolled over the hills, a primal summons, a declaration: *the world has changed.*

The pack answered, their howls weaving together into a single voice of fear, awe, and bloodthirst.

"It is him," Ian growled when the echoes died. "The Orin blood. The boy."

From the shadows, Lyn Brie, a young she-wolf with fire in her eyes and rebellion in her stance, stepped forward. Her fur gleamed in the moonlight, her voice sharp and daring. "I feel him. The pulse of his Geomancy sings in my bones. But it is no tribal song—it is chaos, pure and untamed. He is the full moon's howl, not the pack's."

Ian's gaze was grim, unblinking. "Chaos can be bent. The boy must be brought into the fold. His power must serve us—or it will devour us."

A rumble of agreement coursed through the circle, but one voice cut across it—low, steady, and ancient. Solin Dernier, elder of the tribe, stepped into the moonlight. His fur was streaked with gray, his presence heavy with wisdom. "The child's scent is not wolf alone," he said, his voice rough with age. "It carries the taint of human... and the shadow of betrayal. Bryn walks beside him. The lone wolf who turned from us. The one who follows the Geomancer woman."

A growl spread through the circle, deeper than hunger. Bryn's name was poison to them. His kinship to the boy, his betrayal of the pack, and now his alliance with Bella—the human whose presence they despised—all of it was too much.

Ian bared his teeth, his voice like thunder. "He has chosen a human's heart over the packs'. He has forgotten his blood. He is a traitor." He slammed a clawed hand against the ground, sending dirt flying. "And traitors' blood is forfeit."

The pack howled in one voice, their cry carrying across the night—a vow of death, a vow of reclamation.

Above them, the moon blazed brighter, as though watching, as though judging. And in its cold light, the path was clear: the Geomancers had fallen, the vampires lurked like carrion at the Sanctum's gates, but the pack would not be outdone. They would march. They would claim the Lunar Geomancer as their own.

And they would tear down Bryn and Bella for daring to stand in their way.

CHAPTER THIRTY-FOUR
THE CALL OF THE MOON

INEVITABLE LOVE

The night of the full moon was always a night of power and primal instinct.

Faustus, born of its essence, slept soundly, his power a gentle, humming chorus to the silver light flooding the shattered Sanctum.

But Bryn could not sleep.

The moon was a siren's call in his blood, amplifying his senses, his strength — and the ache of grief for Orin and Emor. Yet beneath the pain stirred something else, a pull he could no longer deny toward Bella.

Across the chamber, she sat by a cracked window, mending cloth with a faint, blue glow at her fingertips. Moonlight washed over her, silvering her hair, softening the scar on her cheek. She was no longer just a Geomancer, no longer just Faustus's mother — she was a survivor, a quiet flame burning against the dark.

The wolf inside Bryn recognized her. Claimed her.

His heart, long heavy with rage, now beat with a rhythm he hadn't felt since Orin's laughter still filled the air. The truth he had fought to bury pressed forward, undeniable.

He crossed the chamber. She looked up, her blue eyes so like Faustus's, full of a quiet understanding. She did not turn away.

"Bryn," she whispered — a question, an answer, and a surrender all at once.

He touched her cheek, gently, reverently. A warrior's hand trembling with something human. She leaned into his palm, closing her eyes as a tear glistened in the moonlight.

The dam broke.

Their lips met, not with the cautious tenderness of new love but with the raw hunger of two broken souls clinging to life. It was a kiss of grief, of defiance, of a love that had no right to exist but burned brighter because of it.

Bryn pressed her against the cold stone, his lips trailing along her neck, and Bella's mind reeled. Orin's voice, Orin's warmth — the memory pierced her even as Bryn's strength anchored her in the present. She opened her eyes, caught between past and present, loss and survival, yet she did not stop him. Not this time.

For one fleeting instant, the air itself shifted — a faint tremor, a ripple in the Geomancy around them. As if something, or someone, stirred in their sleep.

But the moment passed.

In the pale glow of the moon, amid the ruins of a Sanctum meant to destroy them, two broken souls found each other. It was not forgiveness. It was not salvation. It was fragile, desperate love — a beginning carved from grief, one that defied all reason, and one the world itself seemed to watch in silence.

CHAPTER THIRTY-FIVE

THE SILENT STORM

HOPEFUL MOTHER

I n the days that followed, a new rhythm entered the shattered halls of the Sanctum. Bella's Geomancy, once a torrent of raw, uncontained fury, had softened into a quiet, steady hum within her. It was more than just her own power now—it was joined by a small, fragile heartbeat. A new life stirred inside her, a secret beacon of hope hidden beneath the scars of her suffering. The thought filled her with equal parts terror and joy. In a world of blood and ash, she carried something pure.

She said nothing of it to Bryn or Faustus, but the truth lingered in her every step, in the protective way her hands sometimes rested over her stomach. For Bella, who had lost nearly everything, this hidden life was a defiance greater than any spell. It was proof that she was still more than a weapon, more than a pawn. She was still a mother.

But Faustus felt it. A Lunar Geomancer could not help but feel the shift in the currents of her magic. The resonance of her power had deepened, carrying with it a warmth, a vibration that was no longer hers alone. To him, it was something foreign, an intruder in the bond he shared with her. Though he said nothing, a cold wariness settled in his young eyes. He was no longer simply a boy reunited with his mother—he was a storm, and now he felt the burden of sharing her light.

Bella ignored the signs. She told herself that he was only adjusting to freedom, only wrestling with the vastness of his gift. When she caught him practicing incantations in the courtyard, she smiled, heart swelling with pride. She wanted to believe in his goodness; in the boy he still was. But then she saw it—a doe, strangled midair by the tightening vines of a tree at Faustus's command. Its eyes bulged, its life drained in silence, as though the forest itself obeyed his fury.

Her breath caught, but she said nothing. *He didn't mean to. It was just an accident;* she whispered to herself. A mother's denial wrapped itself around her heart like armor. She turned away, forcing herself to remember when she was a child, coaxing rainbows from droplets of water, proud and innocent. She would not believe her son capable of cruelty, not yet.

The Sanctum itself seemed to disagree. Its broken stones groaned under Faustus's footsteps. The runes she tried to restore crumbled into dust at his passing. Even the air thickened when he entered a room, heavy with a silent pressure that pressed on the chest like a storm about to break.

One evening, Bella conjured a simple butterfly of light, hoping to remind him of beauty. It hovered between them, glowing softly. Faustus only stared, his eyes flat, unreadable. And then, without a word, the butterfly dimmed, shriveled, and vanished.

Bella's heart sank, but still she reached for him, brushing his hair back with trembling fingers. "You'll learn, my love," she murmured. "You'll see that power is not just for ending, but for creating."

Behind her, Bryn stood silent, his warrior's instincts taut with unease. His hand rested on the hilt of his blade, not in readiness to strike but in grim acknowledgment of the truth: Faustus was no longer just a boy. He was a storm contained in fragile skin, a storm that even love might not hold forever.

And yet Bella clung to her hope. She had to. If she lost it, she feared she would lose her son altogether.

Child Within

The silence was worse than any tantrum. Faustus drifted through the ruins of the Sanctum like a ghost, his deep-blue eyes holding the cold, unfeeling light of a Lunar Geomancer. He ate only when food was placed before him, spoke to no one, and ignored every effort to guide his power. The air itself betrayed him—a constant, low thrum of energy that hung heavy and metallic, as though the world were bracing for his next outburst.

Bella and Bryn watched him from the shadows, bound together by the same fear. Their fragile love, born in desperation and lit by the moon, now felt like tinder in the path of a storm. Bella pressed a hand to her stomach, feeling the tiny, vibrant hum of new life within her—a heartbeat that sang softly against the oppressive silence Faustus cast around them.

"He knows," she whispered one night by the fire. Faustus lay curled in the corner, his back to them, motionless but listening. "He can feel it. He feels the baby."

Bryn's jaw tightened. "He's not like other children, Bella. His senses... they go deeper. He can feel life itself. And he thinks you're replacing him."

Tears welled in her eyes. "He's wrong. He's, my son. My first. Nothing could ever replace him." She turned to Bryn, her blue gaze pleading. "He needs to know that."

Bryn's expression softened, though grief still shadowed his face. He had lost too much already—his father, his brother, his pack. And yet here, in the wreckage of the world, he had found something worth protecting. Not just Bella, but the child she carried. The bitterness that had once poisoned his heart was gone, burned away by a fierce, protective love. He was no longer just a lone wolf chasing vengeance. He was a man, a father, and a partner.

At dawn they found Faustus by the cracked window, staring at the bruised horizon. The boy's silhouette was framed by pale light, his shoulders tense, his small frame trembling with power he could not—or would not—control.

Bryn and Bella approached together, step for step, a united front of love and fear. They were no longer a human and a wolf, no longer reluctant allies. They were parents, a family.

"Faustus," Bryn said, his voice low and steady—not the growl of a warrior, but the rumble of a father. "We need to talk."

The boy did not turn. The Geomancy around him thickened, vibrating like the strings of an unseen instrument. The temperature dropped, and a guttural sound—more beast than boy—rolled from his throat.

The air grew heavy, oppressive. The storm that had been building in silence was ready to break.

<hr />

Cracks in the Moon

The morning after their attempt to reach him, Faustus was gone from his corner. Bella found him in the courtyard of the ruined Sanctum, standing amid shattered stone. His hands were raised, fingers twitching with unconscious purpose, and the ground responded to his every thought. Pebbles lifted into the air, shards of rock orbiting him like planets around a star. His eyes glowed faintly, the blue of a calm sea, but there was no calm in the way the earth trembled at his feet.

"Faustus," Bella called softly, her voice trembling. "Come down from there, love."

He didn't answer. A boulder cracked open as though split by lightning, dust swirling in the air around him. Bryn moved closer, his instincts taut, every muscle coiled in readiness. He could feel it—the storm was too close to breaking.

"This isn't training," Bryn muttered. "It's a warning."

The boy's gaze flicked to him at last, and for a heartbeat Bryn thought he saw Orin in those eyes—the brother who had been kind even in the darkest nights. But then the light shifted, hardening into something colder, something foreign.

"You don't understand," Faustus said at last, his voice quiet but resonant, layered with a strength no child should possess. "You think you love me. But the moon shows me what you're hiding. You've already chosen her."

The rocks orbiting him spun faster, sharper, until they cut the air with a whistling keen. Bella stepped forward, her heart in her throat. She could feel the truth in his words—he had sensed the new life within her, and the storm of jealousy it awakened in him was beginning to eclipse everything else.

"Listen to me," she whispered, tears streaking her cheeks. "No one will ever replace you. Not now, not ever. You are my heart."

For the briefest moment, the storm wavered. A pebble dropped to the ground, then another. But Bryn's voice, gruff and unyielding, broke the fragile silence.

"If you want to prove it, Bella, don't coddle him. He has to learn control. Or he'll tear us all apart."

Faustus's eyes narrowed. The storm surged back, shards of stone screaming around him in a deadly halo. His gaze burned into Bryn.

"You're afraid of me," the boy said, trembling with both sorrow and fury. "You don't want to teach me. You want to chain me, like they did."

The ground cracked beneath his feet, a fissure splitting through the courtyard stones. The air grew dense, heavy, humming with a power that threatened to boil over. But then, just as suddenly, the rocks fell. The glow in his eyes dimmed, and Faustus turned his back on them both.

The storm had not passed. It had only been leashed, and for how long neither Bella nor Bryn could say.

Chapter Thirty-Six

THE SCENT OF THE SANCTUARY

BIG BROTHER

T he forest was alive with silence, the kind that carried weight instead of peace. The pack moved as one, shadows among shadows, their paws soft upon the damp earth. At their head strode Ian, a massive, scarred beast whose every step carried the authority of an Alpha. The earth beneath them trembled faintly, but this was no ordinary quake. It was not the wild chaos Ian had once sensed—it was something sharper, more deliberate. A pulse. A storm with a heartbeat.

The boy. The Lunar Geomancer. Faustus.

But it was not only his power that drew Ian's attention—it was the scent that clung to the wind, sharp as a knife. He stopped abruptly, his nostrils flaring. The others froze as one.

The first was the scent of a woman. Human, yet laced with the raw tang of Geomancy. Bella. The second was unmistakably Bryn, his estranged kin. That much was already bitter enough. But then came the third: faint, sweet, impossible to miss. The scent of new life. Of an unborn pup.

Ian's lips peeled back in a snarl, the sound rolling low and dangerous through his throat. Bryn had betrayed them once by siding with a human. Now he had gone further, entwining their blood with hers, spawning something new, something neither wolf nor human. A corruption of lineage. A threat to the very survival of the pack.

Solin, the elder warrior, stepped forward, his silvered muzzle dipping in respect to his Alpha. His voice was grave, each word deliberate. "I smell it too. The boy is of our blood—but the human's blood taints it. Bryn's choice has broken every law we hold sacred. He walks as no kin of ours."

Ian's black eyes burned, fixed on the distant pulse of power radiating from the Sanctum. "This is not just betrayal," he growled. "It is desecration. Bryn has soiled the bloodline of Orin. He has defiled our future. And the human—she carries proof of it within her."

A ripple of fury passed through the pack. Hackles rose. Teeth bared. The air filled with growls that vibrated like thunder in their chests.

Ian raised his head, and his howl broke the night. It was not the cry of a hunter—it was the declaration of a crusade. The pack answered, one voice multiplied into a chorus of rage and resolve.

Their mission was no longer only to claim the Lunar Geomancer child. Their path was vengeance. They would spill Bryn's blood. They would tear down the human who had corrupted him. And they would take the boy—Faustus—not as kin, but as weapon.

The moon above bore silent witness as the pack surged forward once more, their fangs bared, their eyes burning. The Sanctum awaited, but now it was more than a battleground. It was the altar upon which bloodlines would be tested, and only one would endure.

Ian Returns

The air changed first.

It was not just scent—it was weight, a heaviness in the soil, a tremor in the bones of the mountain. Bella felt it as a cold echo under her feet, a resonance that made her blood hum with dread. Bryn felt it sharper, deeper. His wolf blood carried certainty where her human senses only carried unease.

The pack was coming.

And at its head was Ian.

Bryn's face hardened into stone. He turned to Bella, his voice a low rumble meant only for her ears.

"They're here. Ian... he knows. He knows about the baby."

Bella's breath caught, her eyes flashing wide in fear. Instinctively, she turned toward Faustus by the shattered window. But the boy did not move. He stood as he had for days: silent, statuesque, his blue eyes distant, his power a steady, suffocating hum filling every corner of the chamber. He felt the wolves too—but his storm was turned inward, coiling around itself like a serpent, waiting.

The ruin of the Sanctum doors exploded outward in a shudder of splinters and stone. Ian stepped into the hall, the rising sun behind him painting his massive frame in fire. Scars ran across his shoulders like crude scripture, and his black eyes locked instantly on Bryn—not Bella, not Faustus, but Bryn.

Behind him the pack entered, a dozen strong, their glowing eyes a wall of feral light. They did not snarl. They did not lunge. They simply stood in formation, their presence alone a declaration of vengeance.

"Bryn," Ian's voice carried across the chamber like the growl of the earth itself. "You have broken the laws of our blood. You chose a human's heart over your kin. You defiled our line with a mongrel child."

Bryn's hand moved to his blade, his stance wide and immovable as he stepped between Bella and the Alpha. His voice matched Ian's for steel and fury.

"She is my mate. And the children—ours. My family. You will not touch them."

Ian's lip curled, his voice a venomous scoff.

"Mate? She is nothing but human filth—a Geomancer, a corrupter. The one she carries in her womb is an abomination, and the boy..." His eyes flicked toward Faustus. "The boy is chaos itself. A weapon. We will take what is ours and cleanse your stain from our blood."

A hush fell. The pack's low growls built into a rhythm, like drums before slaughter.

Then, from the window, Faustus stirred.

He did not speak. He did not roar. He simply turned, his blue eyes glinting with the pale light of the moon. His power, which had been a low hum, rose to a near-unbearable vibration, making the walls groan and the very air tighten. But then—it stopped. The storm pulled back into him, coiled and restrained.

The pack faltered, unsettled. For all their snarls, they understood one thing clearly: restraint from such power was far more dangerous than its release.

The boy was watching, and waiting.

The Storm Breaks

The shattered hall of the Sanctum was heavy with the scent of wolves and blood. Ian stood at the threshold, his pack arrayed behind him, their fury thick in the air. His eyes locked on Bryn, but the boy felt the gaze as well.

Faustus did not move at first. He sat in stillness by the broken runes, his hands resting quietly on his knees. Yet the air shifted with every breath he drew. The stone beneath his feet trembled, faint dust drifting from the cracks in the ceiling. The broken runes flickered, dim pulses of light racing across their surfaces as if stirred awake by his mood.

Bryn stepped forward, blade at his side, body tense. Bella's hands glowed faintly blue, her fear for her son radiating as much as her magic. The pack snarled as one, their eyes gleaming, waiting for the command to strike.

And then Faustus lifted his head.

The low rumble that followed was not from his throat, but from the stone itself. The air thickened — metallic, heavy, alive. Not destruction, not yet, but the promise of it. The kind of pressure that made every chest tighten, every instinct scream of danger. The wolves faltered for a breath, sensing it.

Bella's voice cut through the tension. "Faustus. It's okay. We're here."

The runes dimmed. The tremors quieted. For a heartbeat, the storm held still. The boy's eyes, so cold moments before, flickered with something else — fear, need, recognition. The walls did not collapse. The ground did not split. But the possibility lingered, unspoken and terrifying.

The storm had not yet been unleashed, but everyone in that hall understood: when it did, the world would change.

The First Stand

Ian's sneer was carved deep with contempt.
"A child and a woman. You have fallen far, Bryn."

His words rolled like thunder, a growl that echoed through the ruined Sanctum. Behind him, the pack answered in kind, a chorus of snarls and low growls, their fury thick in the air. They were not individuals; they were one beast, one will, one vengeance.

Bryn stood tall, though the weight of their hatred pressed against his chest like iron. He felt their scorn, the judgment of his bloodline. He was one against many — but he was not afraid. Not anymore. He was a mate, a father, and his defiance was a shield.

He drew his blade, a heavy, silvered sword of human forging. Its gleam caught the fractured sunlight streaming through the cracked ceiling. "They are my family, Ian," he said, his voice low, steady, dangerous. "And you will not have them."

Bella stepped forward, her hands glowing with a soft, steady blue light. Fear gnawed at her ribs, but it was not for herself — it was for Bryn, who stood alone against his pack. She lifted her chin, her voice ringing like a bell of iron.

"We do not want a fight. Let us be. You have your pack, your home. Let us have ours."

Ian laughed, a sound devoid of joy. "Peace? With a human, a traitor, and a mongrel? Never. The blood of Orin is sacred. I will not watch it fouled."

He stepped forward, massive and scarred, his shadow swallowing the doorway. The pack followed — a tide of fur, teeth, and fury.

Then the ground shifted. Not from Faustus, but from Bella. The shattered stones of the Sanctum rose at her command, stacking and fusing into a wall of rock that sealed the chamber's center. The wolves crashed against it with snarls and claws, but it held. Her magic, once gentle, was now a steady hum of defiance. She was no weapon of chaos, but a shield of life.

Bryn seized the opening. With a roar, he lunged at Ian, silver flashing. His strike bit deep into the Alpha's shoulder, drawing blood. Ian staggered — but only for a breath. His answering swipe was brutal, a clawed arc that tore through leather and flesh. Bryn's body crumpled against the stone, his blade skittering away, his breath shallow.

Bella screamed, her cry splitting the air. Her wall shattered outward, shards of stone slicing into the nearest wolves. The pack reeled — but two slipped through the chaos.

Lyn, fierce and young, circled to flank, while Solin, cautious and ancient, moved with grim purpose. His gaze did not linger on Bella's face. It fixed on her stomach. The Alpha's order was clear: cleanse the bloodline.

"Don't waste time with the boy," Lyn snarled. "Go for her. For the womb!"

The words hit Faustus like a blade.

He had been silent, still, his power a low hum in the stones. But now his gaze snapped to them, his deep blue eyes unreadable. He heard the promise — that the new child, the one his mother carried, the one who had taken her heart — would be erased.

Jealousy stirred. Cold, sharp, unformed.

Lyn lunged at him. Faustus did not lash out with destruction. Instead, a shimmering wall of light flickered between them — an illusion, not a shield. Lyn faltered, instincts confused for a single breath. Faustus slipped aside, his small frame darting past, and with a subtle push of Geomancy, redirected her charge into a column of shattered stone. She tumbled, snarling.

But the redirection left a crack. Solin slid through, silent as a shadow, his claws gleaming as he lunged for Bella.

Bella saw him too late. Her barrier was whole — except for the hole her son had opened.

Her scream tore through the chamber. Bryn, bleeding and broken, stirred weakly, his eyes wide with horror. And Faustus, a child and a Lunar Geomancer both, had made his first choice — a choice of jealousy, deception, and a storm not yet unbound.

CHAPTER THIRTY-SEVEN

A MOTHER'S HORROR

A MISCARRIAGE OF A UNITED FAMILY

The howl of the pack was a mournful and terrible chorus as Bella's scream echoed in the ruined halls of the Sanctum. Solin, a blur of fur and muscle, slammed into her. The Geomantic barrier she had been maintaining, a protective shield of swirling stone, shattered with the impact.

The pain was immediate, a tearing agony that hollowed her from the inside. She felt the warmth, the crimson wetness, and then the cold, terrible silence: the hopeful hum within her—the tiny life she had just begun to love—was gone.

She collapsed to the floor, her body convulsing with grief. Her hands clutched at her stomach, but her eyes searched desperately for her son. She found him, standing only a few feet away. Faustus. Her miracle. Her boy.

But he was not looking at her.

His hands glowed faintly with lunar light, his expression calm, detached—too calm. His gaze lingered on Solin, not her. The boy's stillness was not shock. It was choice. And Bella saw it: the faint, deliberate ripple of his power that had opened the way, the subtle betrayal that had let the old wolf through.

Her mind screamed the truth, but her lips refused it. *No. Not him. Not my boy.*

"Faustus..." she whispered, blood running down her cheek as tears burned her eyes. *Please, don't let this be you.*

But he did not move. His eyes, deep and luminous, held the serene certainty of someone who had already justified the horror.

Bryn, meanwhile, saw only his mate crumpled on the ground, her scream still echoing in his ears. The wound across his own side was forgotten as he lunged at Solin, his fury a living weapon. He had not seen Faustus's trick, only the strike that brought Bella down.

"Bella!" he roared, his voice breaking as his blade tore into the wolf's hide. To him, her grief was the grief of a mother losing a child unborn, nothing more. He did not see the deeper wound—the look in her eyes as she watched her living son stand so terribly still.

Bella clung to the stone floor, every sob a war within herself. She could not tell Bryn, not now. He needed to believe Faustus was still their boy, still their hope. If she admitted the truth—that Faustus had chosen this path, that he had sacrificed what could have been his sibling—then the fragile family they had just begun to build would shatter before it ever had a chance.

So she held her tongue.

She wept for the life she lost. She wept for the life she feared she was losing in Faustus. And Bryn, blind to the deeper horror, fought on with the conviction of a father who believed he was saving them all.

The Dream

That night, after the blood and chaos settled, she dreamed.

In her dream, Faustus was no boy. He was grown, tall, eyes burning with the cold light of the moon. At his side stood a woman whose face Bella could never fully see, always shifting in shadow. But her presence was undeniable—fierce, commanding, close. And between them was a child. A small figure with eyes that glowed faintly blue, half-hidden, clinging to Faustus's hand.

The dream made no sense, yet it pierced her to the bone. She did not know if it was prophecy, a warning, or her grief twisting into visions. But the image lingered: Faustus not alone, Faustus with a woman, Faustus with a child of his own. And in his smile, sharp and cruel, she saw not love, but dominion.

She woke trembling, her heart pounding with a truth she could not name aloud: her son was walking toward a darkness she could not stop.

Bryn did not see. He was nothing but fury, a wolf unleashed. His claws and blade tore through Solin, his vengeance swift and merciless. Lyn faltered at the sight of his wrath and fled into the wilderness. Even Ian, a shadow of rage and disappointment, turned and vanished, leaving behind only the broken echoes of his pack.

The battle was over. The war was not.

Bryn, bloodied but unbowed, staggered to Bella's side. His powerful hands, still trembling with rage, cradled her face with a gentleness that undid her. "Bella," he rasped, voice rough with fear. "The pack... they're gone. We won. You're safe now."

Safe. The word was a cruel lie. She was anything but safe.

Her eyes lingered on Faustus, then back to Bryn—her protector, her mate, the man who would crumble if he knew the truth. And in that moment, she made her decision. The horror would be hers alone to bear. She would bury the truth deep, seal it behind her grief, and let Bryn believe in the lie. For Faustus. For their fragile family.

"Solin... he got to me," she whispered, the words tasting of ash. "He struck me."

Bryn's face hardened, his fury reigniting. "Solin," he growled. "I killed him—but it's not enough. Ian will pay for this. I swear it." His eyes, moments ago lit with feral rage, now softened, filled with desperate love. "Are you... are you going to be all right? The baby..."

Bella shook her head. A single tear slid down her face. The pain of her body was sharp, but the pain of her soul was worse: she had lost one child to a werewolf's claws, and another to her own son's choice.

She did not let Bryn see that truth. She let him believe the easier pain.

As he held her close, whispering promises of vengeance and protection, Bella's eyes sought Faustus again. He did not come to her. He did not speak. He only watched, his blue eyes calm, detached, and unreadable.

The dream returned to her in that moment, vivid and damning. She clung to her lie as a mother clings to breath, whispering to herself that she could save him still—that the dream was only fear. But in her heart, she knew this was the first stone laid on the path toward that terrible smile, the shadowed woman, and the child at his side.

Chapter Thirty-Eight

A New Nightmare

Lord Elden's Patience

I n the heart of a shadowed forest, not far from the shattered Sanctum, Lord Elden stood at the head of his army. A thousand vampires stretched behind him, a silent column of pale faces and still bodies. They were not wild like the wolves. They did not snarl or howl. They were a tide of shadows, disciplined and patient, waiting only for his command.

Elden's smile was thin and cruel. The Geomancers were gone. The wolves, fractured and humiliated, had scattered. What remained inside the Sanctum was a broken werewolf, a grieving Geomancer, and a child. A child who was not truly a child at all.

"They are weak," Elden murmured, his voice a silken whisper that carried through the still ranks. "They are broken. And now, they are ours."

The vampires moved as one. No war cry, no thunderous charge — just a slow, inevitable advance, like a tide creeping inland.

Inside the Sanctum

Bella stirred first. She felt it in the earth beneath her hands — not the comforting thrum of life, but a hollow ache. The ground no longer sang; it recoiled. The cold tang of undeath pressed against her senses, filling her lungs, flooding her mind. She turned to Bryn, who was already rising, grim-faced and bloodied, his silvered blade trembling in his grip.

"They're here," she whispered. "The pack is gone. We're exposed."

Bryn's jaw tightened. He stepped forward, placing himself between the ruin's entrance and the fragile family behind him. His body was battered, his strength diminished, but his purpose was absolute.

And in the shadows of the chamber, Faustus watched.

The Child's Fear

Faustus smelled them before he saw them — the sharp, metallic scent of ancient hunger. It was not like the wolves. The wolves were fury and instinct, a storm of blood and teeth. The vampires were different. Their hunger was cold. Measured. Patient.

And for the first time since his awakening, Faustus felt something terrible. Fear.

He saw his mother, pale and trembling, the echo of loss etched into her face. He saw Bryn, bent but unbroken, sword raised in futile defiance. He saw his family — fragile, finite, exposed. And the fear that clenched his heart twisted, reshaping itself into something sharper, something colder.

A terrible love.

Not love for them, but for the *power* he could wield on their behalf. To protect them was to dominate. To destroy in their name was to rule.

Elden's Invitation

The Sanctum's stones groaned as Faustus raised his hands. They did not explode outward in wild fury but shifted with measured purpose. Blocks of stone rose from the ground in precise lines, forming jagged barricades, reshaping the battlefield into a trap. His power was no longer chaos — it was strategy.

Lord Elden stepped through the ruined doorway, his pale face alight with amusement. He spread his arms, a mockery of welcome. "My child," he whispered, his voice wrapping around Faustus like velvet and chains. "Come to me. You and I will rule this world together."

Faustus's blue eyes narrowed. His answer was not words. It was motion.

The Choice

The ground beneath the first ranks of vampires shifted. Stone liquefied, pulling them down like quicksand, then hardened again with a groan, entombing them in silence. Dust rose in choking clouds. Others pressed forward, only to be met with slabs of stone dropping from above, crushing them to black ash.

It was not a storm. It was not a scream. It was a boy's fear, reshaped into calculated destruction.

Elden watched with a predator's patience, not rage. Even as his soldiers fell to dust, his smile did not fade. He saw no monster here, only potential. The child was a weapon. A weapon not yet tempered.

Behind Faustus, Bella cried out — not in triumph, but in horror. She saw the precision in his movements, the way his eyes glowed not with love, but with cold delight. Bryn did not see it. Bryn only saw salvation in the boy's power.

But Bella knew. Each strike, each coffin of stone, was not born of protection. It was born of something darker. Faustus was not shielding them because he loved them. He was destroying because it pleased him.

CHAPTER THIRTY-NINE

THE SURVIVOR IN SHADOWS

BATTLEFIELD

T he battlefield of the Sanctum fell silent. Dust hung in the air like a funeral shroud, and the smell of scorched stone and bloodless ash clung to every breath. The vampires were gone — a thousand shadows, reduced to silence and dust in the wake of Faustus's fury.

But not all.

From the smoke, Lord Elden stepped forward, untouched. His pale figure seemed almost luminous against the ruin, his black cloak trailing like spilled ink over broken stone. Where others had been crushed, he had moved like water, flowing through the cracks of destruction. Not luck, not chance. Calculation.

He applauded once, slowly, the sharp sound echoing in the empty hall.

"A child," he murmured, his voice a velvet drawl. "And yet not a child at all."

Faustus's Glare

Faustus turned toward him, his deep blue eyes glowing faintly, still alight with the embers of power. His hands twitched at his sides, the ground under Elden's feet vibrating with a dangerous hum. But he did not strike. Something in the vampire's presence, his calm defiance, stilled the boy's hand.

"You killed them all," Elden said, his smile curving into something both amused and approving. "Not for love. Not for family. For yourself. For power."

Bella, still clutching her chest, whispered hoarsely, "Stay away from him!" Her voice cracked with fear, but Elden ignored her.

The Promise

The vampire lord's eyes never left Faustus. "You are no one's son, little wolf-blood. No one's weapon. No one's victim. You are what they fear most — a will unchained."

Faustus said nothing. The silence stretched, heavy as stone, until Elden's smile widened. He stepped backward, into the shadows pooling at the doorway.

"I will not fight you," Elden whispered. "I will not waste what you are becoming. I will watch. I will wait. And when you are ready... you will come to me."

Aftermath

And then he was gone — the air where he had stood folding into stillness, leaving behind nothing but the echo of his promise.

Bryn exhaled heavily, unaware of what had truly passed between them. To him, the vampires had fled, defeated by the boy's terrible strength. He sheathed his blade and looked at Bella, who still stared at the empty doorway, her face pale with dread.

But Faustus remained still, his eyes fixed on the shadows Elden had vanished into. Not fearful. Not relieved. Only thoughtful.

The Dream of Ashes

That night, sleep took Bella not as a mercy but as a cruel descent. Her dreams were not the gentle ones of old fields of wild roses or Faustus's laughter as a babe. They were heavy, clotted things, stitched together with grief.

She stood in a place that was neither forest nor stone, but an endless plain of ash. The air smelled of burnt roses, the fragrance of her mother's garden twisted into something bitter. The sky was dim; the light filtered through shifting shadows.

And there he was. Myr.

Not as she remembered him, not the careful voice of a teacher from her childhood, but a silhouette with eyes like burning coals. He did not smile. He only stared, his presence as heavy as the grave.

"You think your lie will protect them?" his voice rolled like a storm across the plain. "You think silence will keep the boy from what he already is?"

Bella clutched her middle, though in this dream there was no wound, no child. Only emptiness. "He is my son," she said, her voice breaking. "I will not abandon him. I will not see him as a monster."

Myr's shadow leaned closer, the ash swirling around his form. "Your father said the same of you once. He chose silence, and in that silence, cruelty festered. Do you think Faustus will be different? Or will he drink from your grief until there is nothing left of you but ash?"

Bella trembled, shaking her head, but she could not deny the truth buried in the words. She had seen Faustus's cold eyes, had felt the subtle betrayal in the Sanctum.

"You lie to Bryn. You lie to yourself," Myr whispered, his voice a knife in her ear. "But you cannot lie to him. Not forever. His path is already written in the blood of your line. And when he walks it, he will not walk alone."

A shadow passed behind Myr, vague but haunting—a woman's shape, faceless, but cradling a child. Bella gasped, her heart twisting with a terror she did not understand.

Before she could speak, before she could cry out, the dream shattered. She woke with tears on her face, the fire beside her burned low, and Faustus was watching her from the shadows. His blue eyes were calm, unreadable, and for one chilling moment, she wondered if he had shared the dream.

CHAPTER FORTY

A FATHER'S RAGE

FAILURE TO PROTECT YOU

B ryn, his body a broken testament to a brave but futile strike, felt the ground tremble—not with his rage, but with his son's. He saw Faustus's power, a cold, precise ripple of force that turned advancing vampires to ash in the space of a heartbeat. It was nothing like his own feral fury. It was calculated. Terrifying. And yet, in the corner of Bryn's heart, where grief and love wrestled, there was pride.

But pride was fleeting. His gaze fell on Bella. She was slumped against the shattered stone, her face pale, her hands limp in her lap. Her sorrow was a wound deeper than his own. And in her eyes, Bryn saw something he could not name—pain, yes, but something buried, something hidden. A truth she refused to share. And so his rage found a new target: the injustice itself.

He stood. His silvered blade gleamed like a shard of moonlight in his hand, his body shaking but unbroken. He was no longer simply a warrior. He was a mate. A father. A shield. And in his fury, he became a storm.

The vampires that survived Faustus's surge—a ragged knot of shadows too slow to fall—had no chance. Bryn did not wait for them to come. He launched forward, claws and steel together, tearing them apart with raw, primal force. The air filled with their dust, black as coal, scattering in the broken light that streamed through the ruined Sanctum. He was not fighting to win. He was fighting because there was nothing else left to do but destroy.

When the last brute fell, its shriek cut short by silver across its chest, silence descended. Bryn staggered, breath heaving, his sword slick with ash and blood. He turned back to his family. Faustus stood calm, his eyes unreadable, power still humming faintly around him. Bella, pale and unmoving, clutched her side but did not speak.

For a moment, the Sanctum felt like a tomb. Then the first touch of dawn spilled across the ruined floor, painting the devastation in soft gold. Survivors—ragged Geomancers who had hidden during the slaughter—peered from the shadows. Their faces were gray masks of fear. They did not thank Bryn. They did not look to Bella. They looked at Faustus, their silence heavier than words.

Bryn broke it first. His voice, rough as stone, cut the air. "We cannot stay here. The wolves will come again. The bats will not stop." He looked at Bella, his eyes hard but pleading. "I know of places. Kin still loyal to me. It is not safe here."

Bella's reply came only after a long, heavy silence. She touched her scar, then pressed her palm against the stone floor as though listening for something far below. Finally, she nodded. "It has been nothing but war since we came. And this place..." She looked toward the broken walls, her eyes distant with old terrors. "...it has already taken too much from me. Perhaps you are right. We should leave."

The choice hung in the silence like a vow. The war was not over, but for now, they had survived—and survival demanded they keep moving.

That night, when the ruins lay quiet and Bryn finally slept from exhaustion, Bella sat alone by the fire. Its glow played across her scar and hollowed eyes. She looked down at her hands, the same hands that had once cradled a new life within her. The memory was a knife in her chest.

She bowed her head, whispering so softly it was almost a prayer. "I'm sorry... my little one. I should have protected you better."

The silence gave no answer, but she felt it—a hollow space inside her soul where a heartbeat had once been. She placed her palm over her stomach, tears cutting quiet lines down her face.

"I'll carry this for us both," she murmured. "Bryn must never know. Faustus... he must never know."

Her whisper faded into the crackle of the fire, and she pressed her forehead to her knees, rocking gently as though trying to comfort the child who would never be. In the shadows behind her, Faustus slept with the untroubled stillness of a storm paused—but not gone.

Bella shut her eyes. She had lied to keep her family whole, but the truth, raw and unyielding, still burned inside her.

CHAPTER FORTY-ONE

THE ALPHA'S BURDEN

MEMORIES OF AN ALPHA

The forest was silent, but it was not the quiet, comforting silence of a peaceful night. It was the suffocating silence of a grave. After Orin's capture, the Orin tribe was a pack without a shepherd, a ship without a rudder. His absence was a raw, open wound in the heart of their conclave, a grim reminder that the old world was gone and a darker one had begun. The Geomancers, once spoken of in warnings and whispers, were now a present, undeniable threat pressing at their borders.

The pack looked to Emor.

Their Alpha—once the storm and the mountain embodied in flesh—was now a shadow of himself. He had forged his sons into men, shaping them with relentless training, with his wisdom carved into their bones. He had taught them to hunt with patience, to fight with purpose, to lead with loyalty. Now he stood alone, a father who had lost one son to his ambition and another to the cruelty of their enemies. The pain was sharp and constant; a cold blade lodged in his chest. Bryn had left. Orin had been taken. And Emor bore the weight of both wounds in silence.

The Scout Returns

One moonlit night, the silence broke.

A lone scout staggered into camp—Dante Valore, a boy scarcely grown into his wolfskin. His body was a ruin of scratches and blood, his eyes wide with terror that no youth should ever carry. He had been with Orin on that night. He was the only one who had come back.

He collapsed at Emor's feet, a trembling offering of grief and failure. The pack gathered, their hackles raised in anticipation of truth. They did not need words to know what Dante had seen. But Emor, grim and unyielding, demanded it nonetheless with a single look.

Dante's voice was a broken whisper.

"The Geomancers... they came with snares, with nets laced in our own skins. They had traps that sang with magic. They didn't kill him, Alpha. They took him. They... they took Orin."

The Alpha's Vow

A stillness fell.

The pack, already heavy with loss, now trembled under the weight of revelation. Orin was not dead. He was worse. He was a prisoner, a weapon caged by human cunning.

Emor's face, carved in stone, betrayed nothing at first. His grief, his fury, his pride—he buried it all beneath the mantle of Alpha. But those closest to him could feel the shift. His eyes, once weary with mourning, ignited with a cold, unrelenting fire.

He bent low, his massive frame casting Dante in shadow. His voice was a growl sharpened into steel.

"Where?"

Dante's hand shook as he pointed north.

"The Sanctum... a prison of stone and magic. That's where they've taken him."

Emor straightened, his shoulders carrying the weight of both fatherhood and Alphahood. He looked to his pack—not with words of comfort, but with a silent command. The hunt was on.

A Father's War

That night, under the pale eye of the moon, Emor made a vow. He would not bury another son. He would not allow human hands to turn Orin into a weapon against his own kind. He was not only an Alpha now. He was a father with nothing left to lose, and the Geomancers had drawn first blood.

The pack felt it, the shift from mourning to purpose. Their grief hardened into resolve, their fear into fury. Where once they had been a chorus of loss, they were now a chorus of vengeance.

The forest itself seemed to bow beneath Emor's will as he led them northward, his silhouette a grim phantom against the moonlight. The burden was heavy, but he bore it with unyielding certainty. For Orin. For Bryn. For the bloodline of wolves that would not break.

The Alpha was no longer waiting for war. He was bringing it to their gates.

The Ghost of a Home

Bryn moved through a world of blinding ice and silent snow, a grim shadow against the pale light. He was no longer just a wolf. He was a lone wolf—honed by solitude, vengeance, and a strength the pack could never have taught him. Once, his name had been a whisper of fear in the hearts of his enemies. Now, he was a storm of cold, beautiful precision. Yet beneath that storm, buried deep, lingered the faint ache of what he had left behind: a home, a brother, a family.

High in a mountain pass, he stumbled upon a Geomancer outpost. Cold, clinical walls of steel and wards carved into the frozen earth stood against the night. Bryn struck like a phantom. The guards fell with silent efficiency, his father's silver-tipped blade flashing in the moonlight. Within the command tent, among ledgers and maps, he found their designs—schemes to bind primal power, to chain what they feared but could not master.

And in the stillness, Bryn heard it. Not a voice, but a whisper carried by the wind:

"A lone wolf is a dead wolf."

His father's words. Forgotten, yet now sharp as a fresh wound. He had left to become a storm. But storms without direction only destroy. In seeking power, he had abandoned the heart of his strength—his pack, his brother, his home. Fury, once his constant companion, ebbed away, leaving in its place a raw and humbling clarity. He was not just a warrior of vengeance. He was a son. A brother. And he needed to return.

The journey home was relentless. Days blurred into nights as he ran, his body moving with mechanical precision, every stride a prayer for redemption. But when at last he reached the familiar clearing of his pack's den, dread struck harder than any blade.

The camp was empty. The fire pits cold, the caves hollow echoes of laughter and life. No blood. No bodies. No struggle. They had not been slain—they had vanished. The home he had once known was not a sanctuary. It was a grave.

Bryn sank to his knees, running calloused fingers through the cold ashes of a long-dead fire. The silence pressed down on him, heavier than any enemy's hand. His heart became a hollow void. He had returned, only to find nothing waiting.

"Bryn?"

The voice was fragile, trembling, like a ghost called by memory. He whirled, blade ready, and froze. From the shadow of a great oak stepped Alina Priya—a werewolf of his youth, one he had once hunted beside. Her face was pale with grief, her eyes wide with unspoken terror.

"Alina," Bryn rasped, his voice breaking like gravel. "What happened?"

Tears welled in her eyes. "Orin... he was taken. The Geomancers came with their runes and their nets of wolfpelt. They bound him in lies and magic. They dragged him away."

Bryn's breath caught, sharp and painful. His brother. His twin. His other half—gone.

"And Father?"

Alina turned toward the empty caves, her grief hardening into fury. "Emor would not abandon his son. He gathered the few who remained. He led them north. To the Sanctum."

Her voice faltered then, softer, as if the memory itself carried shame. "There was... a girl. One of theirs. She came with the guards. Dark-haired, young. I don't know why, but Orin's eyes lingered on her before they forced him into the nets. As though he knew her—or wanted to."

The words struck like an arrow. A girl. A Geomancer. Bryn's heart twisted with confusion and dread. His brother's capture was already a wound; the thought of a connection between Orin and one of their kind was salt poured into it.

The truth, a cold, unyielding reality, settled on him. He had not just come home to an empty den. He had come home to the shadow of a deeper entanglement. His father's fury, his brother's fate, and his own absence were all threads in a web that led to the Sanctum.

The lone wolf who had sought power now stood in the ashes of home, faced with the terrible truth that his most important battle was the one he had abandoned.

The Lost Alpha

The years had not been kind to Emor. Time carved him down to bone and resolve—a weathered silhouette prowling a landscape of half-remembered trails and burned-out campfires. Once an alpha who led with iron and an unbending pride, he had become something harder to read: a hunter whose prey was time itself, whose every step traced the absence of a son.

The pack that remained with him was a ragged thing: hardened warriors with too many ghosts in their eyes. Where once there had been a chorus of howls and story, there were now sparse embers of loyalty, loyalties worn thin by loss. They sheltered in a cave carved from the living rock, a temporary den that smelled of wet stone and old grief. The world outside moved on; inside, Emor's life had narrowed to a single, blunt purpose—find Orin.

Around a dying fire the pack gathered, faces lit by the sputtering orange. The scent of Bella—earth-sweet and strange—hung in the air like a question. She was a human; she moved through Geomancer halls. She had access the pack had never had. To some, that access made her a weapon. To others, she was a wound.

Terrek stepped forward, muscles braced, voice low and hard. "She walks the corridors of their prison twice a week. She brings food, she sees them. She smells like them. If Orin is there, she knows where he is." His teeth flashed in the firelight. "She's the enemy. We should end her and be done."

The sound that followed was not unanimous. Old hunger answered young hatred—growls that tasted of revenge. In the pack's bones, the law of blood was a living thing. But not every throat bared in agreement. Solin, grayer and quieter than the rest, shifted his weight, the old caution in him a slow, steady drum.

"The Geomancers are cunning," Solin said, voice aged by winters and careful thought. "They use wards and silver and guile. They do not take prisoners by chance. If they have Orin—if they keep him for a purpose—then striking blind will only cost more lives. We cannot meet stone with tooth alone."

Around Solin, faces hardened into lines of calculation. Rage wanted a throat to bite; strategy wanted a map. Emor listened. He felt the spear of Terrek's hatred and the slow, practical cold in Solin's counsel. He thought of his son—of the hollow where Orin's laugh had been—and of the long trail that led him here, full of human cunning and dead ends. He thought of Bella: a single human thread that might be the only map through the Geomancers' maze.

He rose then, the cave's shadow falling behind him like a cloak. The pack fell silent. Emor's voice came out like flint. "I will not cast away the only lead we have," he said. "Orin is more than vengeance; he is our blood. We will use what we must to bring him home."

Terrek's eyes flared. "Use? You mean—?"

"—we use the knowledge, not the blade," Emor cut in. "We make her serve the hunt. We do not slaughter what little path remains to our son. If we kill her now, we kill our last chance."

A hiss of discontent ran the circle. Some wolves wanted blood first, answers later. Emor's jaw tightened; the cave seemed to hold its breath. He understood their hunger. He had taught them to burn for retribution. But the hunger that had kept him going all these years was not merely to kill—it was to reclaim what the Geomancers had taken.

· "So she will not die," he said finally. "She will be used as our map. We will move fast, strike true, and take back what is ours. Any who would break that plan for blood will be the ones I answer to."

Terrek's snarl was a living thing, but the pack bowed to the voice of the one who had carried them through worse storms. They would follow Emor, because he had been their mountain; because even a broken mountain can topple empires when it moves.

When the council broke, men receded into shadows, plotting and packing. Solin lingered by the dying fire, eyes on Emor. "You are letting her live because you need her," he said quietly.

Emor nodded once. "I am letting her live because I will not bury my son twice—once in the earth, once in the bitter satisfaction of our rage."

Outside, the night closed around the cave like a fist. Above, the sky was thin and bright with cold stars. Emor stood alone for a long moment, feeling age and hunger in equal measure. The road ahead would require cunning the pack had seldom practiced; the hunt would need patience that felt foreign in their blood.

A lead was a small thing—one human, one scent thread through a tangle of Geomantic lies—but it was a lead. For Emor, a father worn down to the marrow, it was enough.

They would go after Bella. They would bring her to the Sanctum's shadow and make her show the way. The pack swore oaths that night—oaths to blood and bone and to the son that might yet be brought home. Emor, who had become a legend of grief and surety, tightened his fists and let the vow sit heavy in his heart.

Somewhere beyond the cave, distant and blind to the small fires and sharper plans below, the world waited—cold, and patient, and ready to be remade.

A Shared Vengeance

It was harder than they had imagined. Bella moved in and out of the prison under guard, always at the same hours, always calm, always carrying bread. The pack, watching from the trees, grew restless.

"What a cruel Geomancer," Terrek muttered one night, his voice sharp with contempt. "She leaves smiling after feeding those cages. She must enjoy it."

They studied her routine for weeks—the watch rotations, the brief lapses in vigilance—waiting for the perfect moment. But then, on a full moon, something changed.

A hooded figure slipped into the prison. The stride was Bella's. The scent was hers. But the timing was wrong. She stayed far longer than usual.

When the figure finally emerged, hours later, the pack was unprepared to strike. Their chance vanished.

"What was she doing in there so long?" Emor growled, his voice thick with suspicion. His scarred hands clenched until the knuckles whitened. "Did she poison my son?"

The question hung heavy, unanswered.

Days passed, and then the Geomancer fortress stirred with unusual activity—scouts rushing in and out, guards doubling their posts. When Emor's wolf-scout returned, his face was pale with dread.

"Orin," the boy whispered. "They say he is to be executed."

The pack's howls rose like a funeral dirge. They were out of time. Whatever their hatred for Bella, she was their only tether to Orin's cell.

They prepared to strike.

But before they could move, they saw Bella herself taken into the prison, flanked by two Geomancers. She disappeared into the same stone labyrinth as Orin. Hours later, word spread across the campfires like wildfire: Orin was dead. Executed.

Emor did not weep. He could not. His grief had been beaten into steel long ago. Instead, he carried on—relentlessly hunting, endlessly striking at Geomancer patrols—but his pursuit had hollowed him. He was no longer Alpha, no longer even wolf. He was a man with one purpose: vengeance.

It was vengeance that led him to the cave where Bella hid. Her scent was unmistakable—a faint trace of stone-magic beneath the sharper, wilder note of blood.

Inside, he found her huddled in the corner, hair matted, hands trembling. Her blue eyes, wide with terror, were the eyes of prey. She clutched a sharpened stone like a child with a toy.

To Emor, she was no Geomancer at all. She was a broken girl—and yet, beneath the fear, he caught another scent. Faint, sweet. The scent of young blood.

A child. His son's child.

The mountain of a man lowered his weapon. His fury burned, but he swallowed it down, forcing it into silence. If she had Orin's child, then she was the last living link to his bloodline.

"Speak," he said, voice like gravel breaking in his chest.

Bella stammered through her terror. "They... they used him. My son. Your Orin. They turned him into a weapon. And now... now they'll do the same to his child."

Her words were daggers. Emor had seen Geomancers drag children from cages before. He had never dreamed one of them was his grandson.

Before he could respond, the cave filled with low growls. Wolves, a tide of fur and rage, surged inside. Terrek led them, his eyes alight with the lust for blood.

"I knew we smelled filth," he spat, glaring at Bella.

Emor stepped forward, placing his massive frame between her and the pack. His voice was a snarl. "Hold."

The wolves roared in unison, their fury shaking the stone. They would not be denied vengeance.

The Gathering of Wolves

The growls were cut short. A shadow filled the mouth of the cave. The air shifted, heavy with authority.

Bryn. The lone wolf, the storm turned to steel, stepped into the firelight. The pack's howls withered into silence. Their snarls died in their throats. One by one, their eyes lowered.

They had not expected him to return. But now, faced with the phantom of a man they once called brother, they parted like water before a blade.

Bryn walked into the center of the cave, his eyes, a grim, unyielding fire, fixed on Bella. He was a phantom whose name had become legend, his very presence a promise of vengeance.

He looked at Emor, his father, a mountain eroded by years of grief. In his eyes, Bryn saw the reflection of Orin—his twin, his other half. The truth settled like a weight in his chest: he had come home too late.

"Father," he said, his voice low, steady. "The Geomancers... they took him."

Emor's reply was the sound of stone grinding against stone. "They took him, son. They took your brother." His eyes flicked to Bella, curled in the corner. His voice tightened. "And she..."

Emor hesitated, then gave the truth its name. "She bore him a child. Your brother's child. Your nephew."

The cave went still. Bryn's chest rose and fell like a storm trapped inside a cage. His gaze locked on Bella, sharp as a blade. "So she was the reason my brother died a brutal death?"

Emor stepped forward, cutting off his fury with a hand as steady as bedrock. "Stop. Your brother's son needs his mother. Orin would have wanted it."

Bryn's hands shook, his breath sharp and ragged. Rage warred with reason. He wanted to strike. He wanted to tear. But then—through the haze—came a quieter thought.

The boy was blood. His brother's blood. His blood.

Slowly, painfully, the storm inside him began to lessen.

He looked at Bella again, but this time he did not see a Geomancer. He saw a woman lost, broken, alone. A woman carrying the last piece of Orin.

The hunt, which had once been for redemption, shifted in his heart. It was now a hunt with purpose.

Bring his nephew home.

Lessons of Emor

The three had chosen to travel northwest, following the river that cut like a silver blade between the territories of Geomancers and wolves. The abundance of ancient trees provided them cover, their roots and branches whispering secrets older than memory. For Bryn, each step along the river carried echoes of a childhood long buried echoes of the forest where he and his brother had once grown under the stern gaze of their father.

Across that same river, in the ancestral lands of the Orin tribe, Bryn and his identical twin Orin had been raised not just as boys but as wolves learning to be men. Their father, Emor, was Alpha—a warrior forged in blood and scar, his love for his sons a thing shown not in tenderness but in relentless expectation.

"A wolf's strength is not in its teeth, but in its heart," Emor growled, his gravelly voice a constant rhythm in their days. He made them run until their legs turned numb, taught them to read the wind, to scent the change in air before prey even stirred. He tempered their ferocity with patience, their instincts with cunning.

Yet in the mirror of their identical faces, two different truths grew.

Bryn was the storm: faster, impulsive, a fire that burned without pause. He wanted strength without limits, the power to face not only rival packs but the Geomancers and vampires that loomed like shadows beyond the forest.

Orin was the mountain: stronger, deliberate, loyal to tradition. He bore their father's discipline with a quiet ferocity, believing unity and obedience to the pack's laws were the only path to survival.

Emor saw both gifts, and both dangers. "A storm without direction is just wind. A mountain without a heart is just stone. You must learn from each other." But his words, wise as they were, could not close the widening gulf.

When Emor drilled the lessons of the pack into his sons, Bryn always felt the pressure of tradition like a chain, while Orin carried it like a mantle. Emor's words struck deeper into Orin, who saw loyalty as sacred law:

"Blood is not just bond, it is burden. An Alpha's son carries the pack's heart, even if it crushes him."

Bryn never forgot the way Orin nodded solemnly at those words, even as Bryn himself bristled. It was that night, under a blood-red moon, that Bryn realized his brother's path was already fixed — bound to their father's legacy, even if it killed him.

Now, years later, walking the river with Bella and Faustus, Bryn could still hear Emor's gravelly tone, still see Orin's unyielding acceptance. And though Bryn did not yet know it, that loyalty had not died with his brother. It had taken root in another son of Emor, estranged and watching from the shadows.

The Breaking of Brothers

Under the full moon, the chasm became final. Bryn, restless and defiant, packed a few belongings and claimed his father's silver-tipped blade—a relic of their bloodline. He found Orin keeping watch at the edge of the woods.

"The old ways will not be enough," Bryn said, his voice low but resolute. "I must find strength they cannot teach me hère. When I return, I will be a warrior who can truly protect us."

Orin's face—his own face reflected back—hardened. "The pack is our strength. Father is our strength. A lone wolf is a dead wolf." Yet he did not stop his brother. He knew Bryn's spirit had already left.

That night, Bryn disappeared into the trees. The pack mourned in silence, their grief unspoken but heavy, while Orin bore the weight of expectation alone. Bryn, the storm, had become a shadow wandering the world, while Orin, the mountain, became the sole heir to their father's legacy.

Alone in the Wild

The forest, once a cathedral of kinship, became hostile when faced alone. The silence that had once comforted him with pack-breath now screamed with isolation. He missed the steady rumble of Orin's sleep, the shared joy of the hunt. But there was no turning back.

His first trial came not from vampires or Geomancers, but men. A hunting party stumbled upon his riverside camp—three against one. In the pack, their approach would have been marked long before. Alone, Bryn fought with desperate fury. Two fell to his father's silver blade, but the third left a deep wound burning in his side. Days passed as he lay in a hidden cave, fevered and broken, his brother's words haunting him: *A lone wolf is a dead wolf.*

And yet, he lived.

That wound became his lesson. Patience returned to him, not as his father taught it, but reshaped in solitude. He learned to stalk the way shadows moved across stone, to let silence be his second skin. He grew sharper, colder, his fury tempered into precision.

Becoming the Storm and the Mountain

Months bled into seasons. He crossed mountains that split the sky and plains where the sun baked the earth to dust. He fought men who hungered for power, beasts that lived only in whispered tales, and shadows older than language. His blade became not just a weapon but an extension of his will, each strike honed to cruel perfection.

When at last he stood on a cliff, looking over an unknown land, Bryn understood. He was no longer only the storm, raging wild. He had become storm and mountain—relentless, immovable, unstoppable. But he was also alone. The warmth of the pack, the bond of his brother, the wisdom of his father—all were ghosts now.

He had found the strength he sought, but at a terrible price: the storm no longer had a home to return to.

And so his path bent, as all rivers do, toward the Sanctum—toward Bella, toward Faustus, toward the destiny that would one day demand the storm's final reckoning.

The Shepherd and the Snare

The silence of the forest, once a comfort, pressed on Orin like a suffocating cloak. Since Bryn's departure, he had been more than a warrior; he had become a shepherd without a flock, yet the duty was his to bear. His father's voice was still with him, every word a commandment carved into his bones:

A mountain without a heart is just a stone.

Orin was the mountain, the unyielding protector. He had chosen loyalty over ambition, duty over freedom. Bryn's absence carved a hollow in his chest, a wound that time did not close. Still, Orin carried no resentment. His brother was the storm, untamable and wild, and storms could not be caged. Orin accepted his role—to endure, to stand, to guard.

But threats no longer lingered on the edges of rumor. The Geomancers had begun to reach into the wolves' domain. Their presence was not carried by scent or sound, but through an unnatural vibration in the earth, a resonance that unsettled the marrow. They were no longer simply scholars of stone; they were predators, moving with cold, clinical intent.

The Trap

On a moonless night, as Orin led a small hunting party near the borders, the forest betrayed him. A flash of light, a flare of runes woven into wolf pelts, and the air itself turned hostile. The ambush fell with precision, not savagery. Nets laced with sigils ensnared limbs and throats, their pull merciless.

The wolves fought like a storm unleashed, but against sorcery crafted to break them, their strength faltered. Orin, a living monument of his father's training, roared with primal fury. He fought with teeth, with claws, with every ounce of cunning passed down through generations. Yet every strike, every tear of his muscle, was answered by the cold hum of stonebound magic.

Then came the whistle—a keening, high-pitched note that split the night. Its resonance shook his skull, unraveling thought and fury alike. The scent of *lunar elixir* flooded his senses, choking out the moon's blessing, dulling the fire in his blood. His knees hit the ground. His lungs felt caged. His strength bled away until he was left powerless, tangled in nets of his own kind's skin.

The Geomancers did not kill him. They bound him in silence and shadows, dragging him into their sanctum of stone—a trophy, a weapon to be bent, a lure to others.

The Cell

The days that followed blurred into endless gray. The walls hummed with suppressing wards, each pulse draining his essence until he felt hollow, less wolf than shadow. He saw no faces, only hands—cold, impersonal—sliding trays through the slot in his door.

Until one day, the hands changed.

They were smaller, gentler. A faint scent drifted with them—not of iron or spellcraft, but of fresh earth after rain, of life untouched by cruelty. He looked up, and through the slot saw a pair of blue eyes, wide and luminous, framed by a face too young to belong in a place of such desolation.

Dark hair, bound carelessly back, framed her pale features. Though the hum of Geomancy clung to her, it was faint, almost dormant—nothing like the oppressive control of the wardens. She was fragile and out of place, like a wildflower growing through a crack in stone.

Her voice was barely a whisper.

"I'm Bella. My duty is... to feed the prisoners."

The Rose Among Thorns

Orin stared at her, silent. He knew better than to see humanity in Geomancers; their kind were the architects of his torment, the thieves of his strength. Yet this girl—this Bella—was different. In her eyes he found not cruelty, but sadness. Not control, but compassion.

Day after day, she returned. The trays came with quiet words, fleeting glances, the soft cadence of a voice that did not belong in this place. She was no captor. She was a stranger to the cruelty around her, and her kindness, though small, cracked the stone around his heart.

Orin had been a mountain, immovable and unyielding. But for the first time since his capture, the mountain stirred. A new resolve formed within him—not born of vengeance for his pack, but of a fierce, protective need.

He was a prisoner still, but no longer without purpose. He would endure the walls, the pain, the silence. He would escape. Not only for his people. Not only for himself.

But for the rose that bloomed in the darkness.

Orin and Bella

The cell was cold stone and silence, but when Bella appeared, Orin's world shifted. Her presence was like the faintest shaft of moonlight through the cracks of his prison—a warmth he hadn't felt since Bryn left his side.

At first, she said little. She slid the tray through the slot and lingered a moment longer than the others ever did. Her eyes betrayed her: wide, full of unspoken thoughts, not hardened like the wardens'. Orin noticed the way she looked at him—not with fear, not with disgust, but with a quiet sorrow that unsettled him more than any chain.

Over time, her silence softened.
"You shouldn't be here," she whispered once, when no guards lingered nearby. "Feeding you, I mean. They don't trust me with much... but they trust me with this."

Her voice trembled, not with weakness, but with a strange kind of courage. Orin studied her, and though his instinct was to remain the mountain—still, unyielding, untouchable—he felt something stirring. She was a Geomancer, yes, but she was unlike the others. Her magic hummed softly in her blood, not sharp or cruel, but muted, like the earth in spring after a storm.

He should have hated her. Yet the more she came, the harder it was to keep the mountain unmoved.

A Dangerous Affection

Orin had no illusions: he was a prisoner, and she was the daughter of his enemy. But when she set down the tray, sometimes their hands nearly touched. When their eyes met, it was as though the walls themselves faded. He began to wait for those moments—the scrape of the slot, the scent of fresh bread, the brush of her presence.

He never spoke of it aloud, but a dangerous thought began to nest in his mind: *if I escape, I will not leave her here.*

It was irrational, even reckless. But in the quiet, with nothing but the drip of water and the hum of wards, Bella became more than a Geomancer girl. She became a tether—a reminder that not all in this stone-bound place were made of cruelty. She was proof that softness could survive among knives.

And in her, Bella found something, too. She saw not just a wolf caged in stone, but a man carved from loyalty and sorrow, his silence heavier than chains. His suffering called to something deep within her.

The Foreshadowing

Neither of them spoke of what was growing between them, but the seeds had been planted. In the cold heart of the Sanctum, where cruelty reigned, an unlikely bond was taking root. It was fragile, dangerous, and unspoken—but it was real.

What neither of them knew then was that this bond, born in silence and shadows, would one day fracture lives. For Orin, it would become a reason to endure. For Bella, a reason to question everything she'd been told. And for Bryn—though he did not yet know it—it would one day become a wound deeper than any blade.

CHAPTER FORTY-TWO

A QUIET HEARTBREAK

BROKEN FAMILY

T he silence that fell upon their cave was heavier than any storm. The wolves had been driven back, but the victory left only ashes in its wake. Bryn felt it keenly: not triumph, but hollowness. His warrior's instincts told him the danger was gone for now, yet his heart whispered of another kind of peril—the kind that grew in silence and festered in shadows.

He found Bella staring at the horizon, her shoulders slumped, her eyes fixed on nothing. She looked older than he remembered, her beauty veiled by grief. She was not the girl he once distrusted, nor even the woman who had fought beside him. She was something different now wounded, wearied, yet unbroken.

He knelt beside her, taking her small, trembling hands in his rough, scarred ones. "Are you hurt?" His voice was gravel and smoke, steady but inadequate.

Bella's gaze, heavy with sorrow, met his. "The blow was too great. The magic... too strong. We couldn't save him, Bryn."

Her words cut deeper than any claw. Bryn had known wounds of flesh, but this was different. This was the wound of a future that would never be. He bowed his head, his throat thick, unable to speak.

But Bella's silence held more than grief. She could still see it—the wolf charging, the flash of claws, the moment when Faustus could have acted. He had seen, he had known, and he had chosen to let it happen. Her son had watched her unborn child die. And though her heart screamed the truth, her lips could not. How could she tell Bryn that the boy they both protected was the true monster in their midst?

Bryn, oblivious to the silent storm within her, pressed her hands more firmly. "The child..." His voice cracked. "Our child."

Bella lowered her gaze. "Gone."

He pulled her into his arms, a broken fortress shielding a broken heart. For him, it was the loss of hope. For her, it was the loss of trust.

What Fools are We?

Faustus approached them quietly, his steps unnervingly measured for a boy his age. He placed a polished stone into Bella's hand—a silent token. His blue eyes, luminous with an ancient, unsettling light, lingered not on her but on Bryn. For a fleeting heartbeat, Bryn saw not a child, not even a nephew or son, but a rival presence—something powerful, inscrutable, inevitable.

The three of them sat in a triangle of grief. One clung to love. One clung to lies. And one, the boy at the center, clung to power.

The cave's silence soon became a cage. The crackle of firewood, the whisper of wind, all were drowned by the low, relentless hum of Faustus's discontent.

One night, it broke.

"We are fools," Faustus said, his voice carrying weight beyond his years. The stones in the walls trembled at his words. "We hide like rats while the world waits to devour us. We are not victims. We are a weapon. A Lunar Geomancer. We should be kings."

Bella's sewing needle froze mid-stitch. Her eyes brimmed with quiet sorrow as she whispered, "We are not kings, Faustus. We are a family. Power is not what makes us whole."

"Family?" he scoffed, his voice sharp as a blade. "Our home is rubble. Our blood is cursed. The Geomancers and vampires are laughing while we cower in the dark. Why should we not make them fear us?"

Bryn set his tools down, his broad frame leaning forward, his voice deep with warning. "War is no crown, boy. I've lived it. It strips everything from you—hope, love, even your soul. We fight to survive, not to rule."

Faustus's lips curled, his young face shadowed by something colder than moonlight. "You are weak. Both of you. You fear what I am meant to become."

The firelight flickered across their faces: Bella's lined with grief and unspoken truth, Bryn's carved with sorrow and weary resolve, and Faustus's cast in angles of ambition and disdain.

The true war was no longer beyond the cave. It had begun inside it—over the heart of a boy who was no longer entirely theirs.

The Weight of Silence

The cave had become their refuge, a fragile nest of stone and shadow. The fire burned low most nights, its embers crackling against the silence. Outside, the forest whispered with life, but within those walls, silence reigned—not the silence of peace, but the silence of wounds left unspoken.

Bryn mended the silver-tipped blade in silence. Bella wove bandages from torn cloth. Faustus sat apart, his pale hands resting on his knees, his gaze fixed not on his family but on the patterns he carved into the earth. The runes shimmered faintly with Geomantic power, pulsing like a heartbeat only he could hear.

Bella's eyes lingered on him. Once, she had known that look in another man—her father. She remembered the stillness in his eyes before cruelty was done, the cold certainty that power existed to be wielded, not questioned. She shivered, not from the chill, but from recognition.

Defiant Son

Faustus's Subtle Defiance

"Faustus," Bryn said at last, his voice low and steady. "Come closer to the fire. Warm yourself."

The boy didn't move. His lips curled into a faint, almost mocking smile. "I am warmer than fire." He pressed his palm to the ground, and a ripple of heat shivered through the stone, sending sparks up the cave wall.

Bryn's brows knitted, but instead of rebuke, his tone was laced with awe. "Your control grows sharper every day. The earth listens to you."

Bella flinched at those words. Control? No. She saw not control but arrogance, a creeping hunger that disguised itself as mastery.

Faustus finally rose, his shadow stretching long in the firelight. "Fire dies. Stone endures. Fire consumes. Stone remembers. Which would you rather be, Father?"

Bryn did not answer. His silence was a shield, unwilling to admit his unease. Bella, however, heard the venom beneath the boy's words, the subtle rejection of warmth, of family, of love.

A Mother's Nightmare

That night, Bella dreamed.

She stood in the Sanctum's ruined halls, but they were whole again—gleaming walls of rune-etched stone. In the center, her father loomed, his hands dripping with blood. Behind him, Faustus stood, taller, older, eyes burning with the same cruel light.

"You thought one curse was enough," her father whispered, his voice a blade cutting through her. "But your blood carries the seed. You bore him, Bella. You gave my legacy flesh."

Faustus turned toward her, his face half-shadowed, half-radiant with the cold light of the moon. In his arms was a child—his child—its eyes like pits of silver flame.

She reached out, screaming, but the dream shattered before she could touch him.

A Growing Rift

She awoke with a gasp, sweat chilling her skin. Beside her, Bryn slept heavy, the exhaustion of battle sinking him into silence. Faustus, however, was awake. He sat at the cave's mouth, watching the forest, his profile carved in moonlight.

Bella rose quietly, wrapping her cloak around her. "Faustus," she whispered.

He didn't look back. "The world waits, Mother. It waits for me."

She froze. "Waits for what?"

"For the storm." His voice was calm, detached, terrible. "And storms do not hide in caves."

The Fire and the Fang

The forest had been uneasy for days. Animals moved in strange patterns, and the wind carried scents Bryn could not name. His instincts warned him before the sound reached his ears: the soft thrum of feet in the underbrush, the deliberate rhythm of hunters. Vampires, lean and restless, had tracked them again.

Bryn rose at once, silver blade in hand, his body tense and ready. He looked to Faustus, expecting fear or hesitation. Instead, he found his son already standing at the cave's mouth, eyes alight with an eerie silver glow.

"They are not hunters," Faustus said flatly. "They are prey."

The first vampire lunged from the shadows, a blur of teeth and claws. Bryn moved to intercept, but Faustus was faster. He whispered a wordless command to the earth, and the ground split like parchment. A jagged stone spike erupted beneath the creature, impaling it before it could land. Its body turned to ash before it hit the ground.

Bryn froze. The kill had been efficient—too efficient. Yet pride surged through him, fierce and unyielding. "You move like a warrior born," he growled, his voice low with admiration. "Your enemies won't know fear until they see you."

Faustus tilted his head, his lips curling in the faintest smile. "Fear is not enough. Fear fades. I want them to kneel."

A Mother's Dread

Bella saw what Bryn could not. The boy's face was not lit with courage, but with hunger. Each strike of his power was not defense but indulgence. He reveled in the destruction, and with every vampire that fell, his smile grew colder.

Another wave came, hissing through the trees. Faustus raised both hands, and the forest obeyed him. Branches twisted into spears, roots lashed out like serpents, snapping bone and tearing flesh. The night filled with the sound of breaking bodies, not the chaos of battle but the orderly rhythm of slaughter.

"Faustus!" Bella cried, her voice sharp with terror. "Enough!"

For an instant, his power faltered. The branches froze mid-strike, the roots recoiling like wounded animals. His eyes flicked toward her, wide and wounded—but the moment passed. The roots struck anyway, finishing what they had begun.

The vampires lay in heaps of ash, their threat extinguished. The forest grew still again, but the silence that followed was heavier than the fight.

The Rift

Bryn clapped a hand on Faustus's shoulder, his face split by a rare smile. "You fought like a true Alpha's son. Like your uncle."

But Bella could not smile. She saw not victory, but prophecy. In her dreams, she had seen this before: her father, her son, the same hunger reflected in their eyes.

Faustus stood between them, his body taut with pride and defiance. He looked at Bella with an expression she could not name—part longing, part accusation. "You want me to hide what I am. But I am not just your son. I am the storm."

Bryn tightened his grip on the boy's shoulder, mistaking defiance for courage. "Then let the world beware."

Bella turned away, her heart breaking under the weight of a truth she could never speak aloud: the storm would not protect them forever. One day, it would consume them.

The Dreaming Hollow

The forest lay quiet after the battle, but Bella could not sleep. Bryn's heavy breaths filled the cave, his body finally yielding to exhaustion. Faustus sat near the embers, his silver eyes reflecting the dying fire, unreadable, unblinking. Bella turned on her pallet, her body still aching, but it was her mind that throbbed most. She closed her eyes, but rest did not come. Instead, the dreams returned.

She saw her father again. His face, stern and lined with years of pride, towered over her like a shadow that would never fade. His voice was a cold whisper, echoing through her dream: *"There must not be another like you. No child must rise to rival you."* She remembered the blood, her mother's cry, the cold gleam of steel. He had stolen life not from an enemy, but from his own family.

Then, in the dream, the figure shifted. Her father's eyes became Faustus's. The cold determination, the hunger for control — they were the same. She wanted to scream, to deny it, but her voice was lost in the hollow.

Myr in the Shadows

Out of the dream's mist came another figure, familiar and dreaded: Myr. The oracle's voice was neither accusation nor comfort, but inevitability.

"Blood repeats itself, Bella. Cycles are the bones of the earth. Your father sought to end what he feared. Your son will begin what he desires. You cannot change it."

Bella shook her head in the dream. "No... he is mine. He is not him."

Myr only looked at her with eyes like glass. "Then pray you are stronger than your mother."

Bella woke with a scream muffled in her throat, her body drenched in sweat. The fire was almost dead, the cave still. Bryn stirred but did not wake. Faustus turned his head, his gaze meeting hers in the dim glow.

"Another dream?" he asked, his voice soft, almost too calm.

She could not answer. She only nodded.

Faustus's eyes lingered on her, unreadable. For a heartbeat, she thought she saw pity — but then it was gone, replaced by that cold gleam again. He turned back to the embers without another word.

Bella curled in on herself, clutching her chest. She knew what Myr meant. The storm was coming, and it was already inside her home.

CHAPTER FORTY-THREE

THE DEPARTURE AND THE HUNT

THE EMPTY DAWN

The morning after the storm of words and silence, the cave was too still. The fire had gone out, leaving only a faint trail of smoke curling toward the stone ceiling. Bella woke first, her body stiff and aching, and the chill of absence fell over her before her eyes adjusted to the dim light. Faustus was gone.

No overturned stones, no blood smeared into the dirt, not even the faint scuff of footprints. Just gone. As though the forest itself had swallowed him whole. Yet Bella felt it—the faint, lingering thrum of his power humming in the earth, a low resonance carried by the morning wind. It was not peace. It was warning.

She sank by the ashes, her trembling hands clutching her cloak. Her heart, already broken from loss, now caved further beneath the weight of terror. *Not again. I cannot lose another child.*

A Mother's Resolve

Bryn stirred from his rest, his body still bruised and torn from battles fought in blood and shadow. He looked at her, the hollow in her eyes telling him everything before she spoke.

"He's gone," she whispered. The words cracked, fragile things carried into the silence. "We can't let him go alone. He'll get himself killed." Her voice firmed with a desperate strength. "We have to find him, Bryn. We can't let the world take him too."

Bryn stood slowly, the weight of his wounds nothing compared to the weight in his chest. He had fought battles for this boy, warred against wolf and vampire alike. But Faustus was not a prize they could guard. He was a force that strained against their grip with every passing day.

Still, Bryn knelt beside her, running a calloused hand through her dark hair. His face was lined with exhaustion, but his voice was steady, grounded. "I know," he said, the words carrying both promise and fear. "We'll find him. We'll protect him. And we won't let them—or him—turn him into a weapon."

The New Hunt

The silence of the cave pressed in around them, but now it was no longer grief alone—it was resolve. The war for Faustus's soul, which had begun in bloodied halls and prison stones, had shifted. It was no longer wolves or vampires at their door. It was Faustus himself, vanishing into the wilds with power burning beneath his skin.

Bryn strapped on his blade. Bella pulled her cloak tight. Together, they stepped into the pale morning light, the forest waiting with the quiet, patient malice of a hunter.

This was not a journey for war or vengeance. This was a hunt for their son.

And this time, they swore, they would not lose.

The Wanderer's Path

The wilderness was quiet, but it was not the silence of peace. It was the silence of a predator's lair, thick with menace and expectation. Faustus moved through it alone, his steps measured, his blue eyes reflecting the pale silver of the moon. Without Bella's whispering reassurances or Bryn's heavy tread beside him, the forest felt sharper. The trees loomed closer, the shadows seemed deeper, and the air itself pressed down with a weight he found exhilarating.

He did not feel lost. He felt free.

Their cave, their fire, their endless grief—it had been a prison. Bella with her clinging love and Bryn with his brooding watchfulness—both saw him as something fragile, something to be shielded. They were fools. He was no child to be hidden away. He was a weapon, and weapons did not hide. They were meant to be wielded.

He remembered Bryn's words about peace, about family. Weakness dressed as wisdom. He remembered Bella's insistence that love was enough to keep them whole. Love—what had love done but shackle her heart and blind her eyes to truth?

Faustus walked because he would not be shackled. He would not bow to their grief, their lies, or their fear. If power was his inheritance, he would not waste it burying himself in the ashes of their sorrow.

The First Test

By dawn, he had wandered into the hunting grounds of a band of brigands. Three men, laughing and drunk on stolen wine, stumbled across him where he crouched at the river's edge.

"A lost boy," one sneered, raising his crossbow.

Faustus turned, calm and still. The ground beneath their feet shifted. Not violently—just enough to send one man sliding into the water with a startled cry. The others laughed, until the bank crumbled further, trapping them knee-deep in sucking mud.

He did not kill them. Not yet. He let them flail, their curses growing shrill as the earth clung tighter, until their fear became a scent he could taste on the air. Only then did he release them, the mud loosening as though mocking their panic. They staggered away, pale and trembling.

Faustus watched them go, a faint smile touching his lips. Not chaos, not wrath—control. This was how a Geomancer's power should be used.

Dreams of Blood

That night, the forest pressed close around him. Sleep came, but not peace.

He dreamed of a woman he had never seen but somehow knew—the faint outline of Bella's mother, broken and fading. Beside her, a man whose eyes burned with the same cold fire Faustus often saw in his own reflection. Bella's father.

The man's voice echoed through the dream, harsh and unrelenting: *There must never be another like her. Sacrifice is the only way to protect what is ours.*

Myr's shadow lingered at the edge of the vision, watching, waiting.

Faustus woke with his heart pounding, a sharp taste of iron on his tongue. He lay still for a long time, staring at the stars through the canopy. He did not understand the dream, not fully. But it left him with the uncanny sense that his choices were not entirely his own. That cruelty ran in his blood like a second inheritance, whispering to him in the silence of night.

Horizon

By the second morning, he had reached high ground. The forest fell away into a vast sweep of plains and rivers, a world sprawling wide and waiting.

For the first time in his life, he did not feel small beneath its immensity. He felt aligned with it, as though the endless horizon had been carved for him.

He clenched his fists, the thrum of his Geomancy running steady beneath his skin. He would not survive. He would not hide. He would claim.

The boy who had left the cave was gone. The Wanderer had taken his first steps.

CHAPTER FORTY-FOUR
VENGEANCE

FAUSTUS

The cold, still air of the morning clung to Faustus's lungs like frost. He moved through the trees with purpose, not the reckless speed of a boy, but the deliberate stride of one who had chosen his path. The shadows bent toward him; the soil itself hummed faintly beneath his steps. He no longer craved his mother's hand nor his father's approval. He was his own weapon now, sharpened by jealousy and honed by loss.

Ahead lay a Geomancer outpost, a fortress of wards and discipline. He felt the prick of their protective magic against his skin—unwelcome, but not impenetrable. He drew a long breath and pressed forward.

The wards did not crumble in an instant. They resisted, each rune a knot he had to pry open, and the effort bled sweat from his brow. Inside, the Geomancers fought back. Their circles flared, their voices rose in practiced unison. For a heartbeat, they held him. For a heartbeat, he thought he might falter.

But his rage surged, and with it, his resolve. He twisted their own defenses inward, cracked the stone beneath their feet, and sent jagged spikes through their formation. Two fell screaming. A third collapsed when the barrier split beneath her weight. The rest fled, their order broken.

Faustus sank to one knee, his breath ragged, his lips streaked with blood. Not triumph, not yet—but the mark of a weapon learning to cut.

Bella and Bryn

Back in the cave, the silence was unbearable.

Bella sat by the cold ashes of the fire, her hands trembling as if she still felt the phantom heartbeat of the child she had lost. Another loss now pressed against her chest like a weight she could not bear. *Faustus is gone.*

Bryn moved like a shadow at her side, his face a mask of sorrow carved into stone. He had searched the perimeter at dawn, his senses straining for pawprints, for scent—anything to tell them which way the boy had gone. There had been nothing. No struggle. No sign of pursuit. Faustus had chosen to leave them.

"He's still alive," Bryn said, his voice a low growl meant to sound certain, but it trembled beneath the weight of doubt. "I can feel it. His blood is ours."

Bella shook her head, her eyes hollow. "Alive isn't safe. Alive isn't ours. You didn't see his eyes, Bryn. He wasn't a child when he looked at me. He was already—" She stopped, her throat closing. She couldn't say *monster.* Not yet.

Bryn crouched, resting a scarred hand over hers. "Then we'll find him. We've hunted before. We'll hunt again. We will bring him home."

But in the quiet that followed, Bella knew he didn't understand. *Home is the one place Faustus does not want to return to.*

Faustus, Later

The boy returned to the Sanctum, no longer its prisoner but its shadow. He moved carefully, his reserves thin. The council chamber's runes pressed against his mind like thorns. He peeled them away, not with a wave of destruction but with steady, gritted patience, until the doors cracked open with a groan.

The elders turned, their faces pale, their voices stammering half-formed incantations. Faustus chose one—just one—and crushed him beneath a rift in the floor. The rest cowered. Their fear filled the chamber thicker than smoke, and Faustus left them alive. Corpses would fade. Survivors would whisper.

As he staggered from the chamber, his body a trembling vessel barely holding together, a bitter smile tugged at his lips. They would carry his name. Not as a god. Not yet. But as something rising.

Bella and Bryn, Closing

That night Bella dreamed of fire. Not the kind that warms, but the kind that consumes. In the dream, she saw her son standing over ruins, not running from them. His hands glowed with the same cold light she had once loved in his eyes.

When she woke, Bryn was watching the cave mouth, sword across his knees, a sentinel carved of fury and love. She pressed a hand to her stomach, aching at the hollow place where hope had once been.

"Bryn," she whispered, her voice breaking. "What if we don't bring him back? What if we only follow the trail of what he leaves behind?"

Bryn didn't answer. His silence was the heaviest truth of all.

The Council Chamber

In the darkness beyond the Sanctum walls, something stirred. Far across the frozen ridges, a pale figure lingered at the edge of shadow. His army was still, his presence hidden, but his senses stretched far.

Lord Elden smiled. Not the smile of triumph, nor of pity, but of recognition. He had felt the tremor ripple through the ley lines, the faint echo of a child wielding power that should not yet be his. "So," he whispered into the night, his voice carried on no breath, "the storm has begun."

He did not move toward the Sanctum, not yet. A hunter never chased before the prey had ripened. But his eyes, cold and luminous as the moon itself, fixed on the broken fortress. Soon. Very soon.

Nightmare

That night, as Bella drifted into an exhausted sleep, her mind—already fragile from grief and lies—was torn open by a dream.

She stood in the Sanctum, but it was not the Sanctum she remembered. The walls bled shadow, the runes pulsed with a sickly, crimson light, and Faustus stood in the center—his eyes no longer blue, but black mirrors that reflected nothing. Around him, the dust of the Geomancers swirled like ash caught in a storm.

A voice rose out of the shadows, not hers, not Faustus's. It was cold, elegant, and ancient—its tone both mocking and strangely tender. *"The storm ripens, and even the mother will break when the son takes his crown."*

Bella turned, but there was no figure, only a tall silhouette at the edge of her vision. Pale hands folded in patience, eyes glowing faintly like coals in mist. She tried to scream, but her voice was swallowed by silence.

She woke with a start, her skin cold, her breath ragged. Beside her, Bryn slept fitfully, the firelight casting deep shadows across his scarred face. She turned to Faustus, who sat awake, watching the flames. For a moment, she thought she saw those same pale eyes from her dream reflected in her son's gaze. She blinked, and they were gone—but the chill remained.

CHAPTER FORTY-FIVE

THE ASH OF ARMIES

THE GREAT VAMPIRE ARMY

F rom his vantage point high above the battlefield, Count Arad
watched with a detached, cruel amusement.
"Ha... ha, ha. Pathetic. Just pathetic."

The Geomancers had been clever using the half-breed boy as
bait, a weapon dressed as a child. The werewolves had walked into the
trap, the Geomancers had prepared their ritual, and all the players were
in place. A perfect game, or so they believed.

But when the storm came, it was not theirs to control.

Arad's amber eyes narrowed as Faustus stepped forward, a figure still young, still unformed, but carrying a resonance unlike anything the world had yet seen. His hands rose, and the ground itself
obeyed. Stone groaned, earth buckled, and the air trembled with a
power that was not Geomancer order, nor werewolf fury—but something fused, something worse.

Lord Elden, supreme among the vampires, had offered the boy a place. A throne. A kingdom of shadows at his side. The boy had answered not with words, but with ruin.

The earth split open. The tightly packed ranks of the vampire host, perfect in formation, became their own coffin. In seconds, centuries of undeath crumbled into ash. The air thickened with the bitter dust of his kin. Elden's court—an army of a thousand—was gone, not with the slow grind of war, but with the sharp, merciless clarity of a single blow.

Arad had lived for centuries. He had seen empires fall and kings bled dry. But never had he seen a power wielded with such cold precision. The boy did not flail or rage. He cut. He chose. He left survivors not out of mercy, but design. A message. *Remember me. Fear me. Carry my name.*

In that cruel pattern, Arad understood: Faustus had spared Elden deliberately.

The Count glanced at his lord. Elden stood still, his pale face unreadable, his robes flecked with the ash of his children. He had ruled for a thousand years through patience and cunning, but in his eyes now was something Arad had never seen before: true fear.

Elden's lips curved, almost a smile, though it did not reach his eyes. "Power that burns this bright cannot burn forever," he murmured.

He would not chase the storm. He would survive it. He would scatter, gather, and wait. When the boy's fire dimmed, when his vengeance wore into weariness, then Elden would strike—not as a ruler of shadows, but as their patient master.

The field below was a grave. The Geomancers' Sanctum, once a prize, was now a ruin. And in the ashes of that army, a new terror walked the world: a Lunar Geomancer, born of two legacies, neither master nor servant, but something far worse.

Arad's lips tightened. The game was not lost. It had simply changed.

CHAPTER FORTY-SIX

THE SANCTUM'S SILENCE

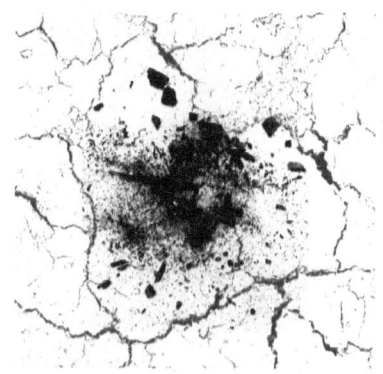

MOVING ON

The journey to the Sanctum was a blur of frantic hope and mounting dread.

Bella's every step was driven by the memory of Faustus's Geomantic beacon—a raw, pulsing signal that had pulled her through the wilderness like a lifeline. Bryn ran beside her, silent as shadow, his movements a grim symphony of vengeance and weary duty. They were not warriors seeking battle, but a mother and father chasing a boy who was already slipping beyond their reach.

At sunrise, the fortress rose before them. Once a bastion of order and reason, the Sanctum now stood as a monument to ruin. The outer wards, which Bella had once believed unbreakable, were gone—erased as though they had never existed. The air, which should have hummed with the steady rhythm of Geomancer magic, reeked instead of iron, ash, and scorched stone.

The gates of ironwood were nothing but splintered wreckage. Waves of raw, untampered Geomancy clung to the walls, fading echoes of a storm too immense to belong to a boy. Bella stopped short, her eyes wide with a terrible certainty.

"He was here," she whispered, her voice breaking. "Faustus did this."

Inside, devastation awaited.

The grand library—once a sacred chamber of lore—lay buried beneath smoldering ash. The ritual halls were cracked and broken, Heartstones shattered into glittering shards. The elders, pillars of the order that had once caged Faustus, were gone, reduced to powder fine as smoke. Yet amid all the ruin, there was no sign of the boy himself.

Bryn knelt among the dust, his hand sinking into the black remains of what had once been living, breathing adversaries. His face tightened, not with triumph, but with dread. "This wasn't a battle," he muttered. "It was a cleansing. He's not our boy anymore, Bella. This..." He let the ash trickle through his fingers. "...this is the work of a Lunar Geomancer."

Bella's throat tightened. She could still feel him—his presence humming faintly through the stones, no longer a frantic cry for release but a steady, cold pulse of intent. The resonance led northward, unmistakable.

"He's hunting," she whispered. "He's following the vampires. Their fear is his guide."

The words sank like stones into Bryn's chest. Faustus had not broken free to return home. He had become a predator. His prey was not a man, not a clan, but an entire army of the undead.

Bryn turned to Bella, his voice rough, almost desperate. "We have to find him. We have to stop him."

She met his gaze, her own eyes hard with a terrible resolve. "No," she said quietly. "We can't stop him, Bryn. Not now. We can only try to guide him. If all he knows is vengeance, he'll burn the world to cinders. We have to show him there's more. We have to remind him of love."

In the hollow ruins of the Sanctum, surrounded by ash and silence, their mission changed. They had come to rescue their son. Now they were chasing something far more fragile—and far more dangerous: the chance to save what was left of him.

The Rebirth of the Sanctum

Bella stood in the center of devastation, her face a mask of weary strength. The scar left by the vampire's strike was a constant reminder of what she had endured, but her hands—once conduits of destruction—were now tools for creation. Closing her eyes, she drew deeply on her Geomancy, not to tear the earth apart, but to mend it.

The shattered stone groaned as if remembering pain, then rose from the floor. Not in a violent torrent, but in a careful, deliberate rhythm. Rubble became walls again. Cracks sealed with molten rock. Fractured Heartstones glowed faintly as she coaxed them into new harmony. The fortress that had once been a cold, unfeeling prison reshaped itself into something new: a living sanctuary, a home of stone and hope.

She was not alone. The spared survivors of Faustus's storm—a handful of low-powered mages and frightened children—watched in silence, then slowly gathered around her. To them, Bella became not a prisoner of their order, but its unlikely teacher. She guided their trembling hands, showing them how to feel the pulse of the earth, how to let its rhythms guide their strength. Where the old elders had prized cold logic, Bella spoke of empathy. Where they had demanded control, she taught listening. The children, bright-eyed and eager, reminded her of a time long ago—before her father, before the forced marriage, before the lies. For a moment, she smiled. But memory was cruel. Thoughts of her father, of

Loryndor abandoning her, came unbidden, erasing the warmth as quickly as it had arrived.

The survivors carried the mark of fear. They had seen the Lunar Geomancer's wrath with their own eyes; their mentors reduced to dust; their traditions shattered in a heartbeat. Bella sought to turn that terror into something gentler. She built not another Sanctum of power, but a refuge of protection. Yet as she worked, her heart remained a battlefield.

The loss of her unborn child lingered like a hollow wound. And beneath her new mask of resolve lay a darker truth—the knowledge of Faustus's betrayal. She saw Bryn, broken warrior that he was, stripped of his father, brother, and pack. She wanted to share it with him, to tell him the full weight of what had been done. But the words never left her lips. The lie became her shield. She bore it for his sake, for hers, and for the boy who had already grown into something the world could not contain.

From the shadows, Faustus's presence was never far. She felt him as a pulse in the distance, his Geomancy no longer wild, but steady and deliberate. He was no longer her son. He was a storm in human form, a predator circling the fragile sanctuary she tried to build.

Bella's war was not against the werewolves. It was not against vampires. It was not even against the remnants of the Geomancers. Her war was against silence, against a lie that chained her to guilt and bound her to a son who was both her greatest love and her greatest fear. Every stone she raised, every child she guided, was a desperate act of defiance. But she knew the truth: the new Sanctum was not just a fortress of hope. It was a fragile shield against the storm Faustus had become.

CHAPTER FORTY-SEVEN

THE ALPHAS'S DEFEAT

REGROUP

The forest was no longer theirs. The retreat from the Sanctum had been a rout, a panicked flight through the night that stripped the pack of dignity as much as numbers. Terrek carried the humiliation in his chest like a stone: the Sanctum he had wanted to claim was now a tomb, his warriors dead in heaps of dust and fire.

They holed up in a cavern cut into the hillside, hidden deep beneath old trees. The survivors huddled close, scarred and silent, a fraction of what had once been a proud hunting force. Around the fire, the council of elders gathered, grim faces marked by age and loss. They spoke little of vengeance now. Their voices circled around one word — survival.

"We hide," Terrek told them, voice like gravel sliding over steel. "We find another den. Another life. The world has shifted. We cannot face what the Geomancers and vampires themselves failed to master. We must outlast it."

The elders, wearied and beaten, bowed their heads. For them, survival was enough. They had seen the Lunar Geomancer with their own eyes. To fight him was to throw themselves into a storm they could never weather.

Yet in the shadows of the cave, younger eyes burned with something else — contempt.

The Rise of Glavius

Glavius Lynch was young, large-framed, and restless. Where others saw a monster too terrible to face, he saw a prize too valuable to waste. As Terrek spoke of retreat and hiding, Glavius stood.

"We cower from a boy," he growled, his voice steady and sharp. "We call ourselves wolves, yet we behave like mice. The Geomancers tried to wield him as a weapon and died. The vampires tried to chain him and burned. We will not repeat their mistakes. We will claim him. His blood is our blood. His power belongs to us."

The cave stirred with uneasy growls. Some elders spat in defiance, but others — the young, the ambitious — leaned toward him.

The challenge came swift, as all wolf challenges do. Terrek met Glavius in the center of the cavern. The Alpha fought with bulk and rage, his claws flashing with the desperation of a leader about to be unmade. But Glavius fought with precision. He dodged, feinted, and cut through the older wolf's defenses until pride left its fatal gap. One strike was enough. Terrek fell, breath gone, body heavy as stone.

The silence that followed was not grief. It was recognition.

Glavius stood over the fallen Alpha, chest heaving, face a mask of resolve. "We will not run," he said. "We will not hide. We will find the boy.

We will show him his place is with us. And with him, we will cleanse this world and take what is ours."

The pack answered not with doubt, but with a howl — low, rising, and eager. A fractured pack had chosen its path, and it was no longer survival. It was conquest.

Terrek's Fight

The forest floor was a map of old struggles and forgotten victories. For Glavius, a young wolf of formidable size and strength, it was also a testament to a way of life that was failing. Born under Terrek's rule, he had never known the pack's former glory under Alpha Emor, only the grim, hardscrabble existence of a defeated people. He was bigger and stronger than his peers, a fact that both isolated him and fueled a quiet resentment. While other wolves spoke of honoring tradition and surviving in the shadows, Glavius's heartbeat with a different rhythm—a deep, unyielding thirst for power.

His ambition was not born of spite, but of observation. He watched Terrek lead with desperation rather than vision, clinging to survival while their enemies carved away at their world. The pack, once hunters, had become prey, losing ground to Geomancer patrols and to the opportunistic vampires lurking at the edges of the forest. To Glavius, the old ways—the endless cycle of flight and fear—were a slow death.

The psychic shockwave from the Sanctum proved him right. That raw surge of power, unlike anything the pack had ever known, was not just terrifying; it was clarifying. The world was changing. There were forces rising—Geomancers, vampires, half-breeds, and now a Lunar Geomancer—that could not be ignored. To Glavius, these powers were not obstacles. They were opportunities. If the wolves could harness them, learn from them, even claim them, then no enemy could stand against them.

His vision stretched further than a single weapon. He saw the wolves not as a dwindling tribe but as conquerors. The forests, the mountains, the human settlements, even the ruins of Geomancer strongholds—all of it could be theirs. The pack had the blood, the strength, and the will. All they lacked was a leader who would not bow to fear.

That leader would be him.

The challenge to Terrek came swiftly. Terrek fought with pride, swinging like an Alpha desperate to hold onto his crown, but Glavius fought with precision and certainty, fueled by the vision of a new order. He struck where Terrek faltered, exposing the weakness of a leader who had already been defeated in spirit. One decisive blow ended it.

Terrek fell, breath gone, spirit broken.

Glavius stood above him, chest heaving, amber eyes burning. "We will not hide in caves," he said to the stunned pack. "We will not run from the Geomancers or bow to the vampires. The world is changing, and we will change with it. We will take what is theirs—power, land, fear—and make it our own."

The pack howled their answer, not with grief but with hunger. They had a new Alpha. One who promised not mere survival, but conquest.

Chapter Forty-Eight

THE CALL OF A KING

THE MONSTER

F austus's mind was not a place of chaotic, unthinking rage. It was a place of profound and terrible clarity. He had just seen the raw, destructive power he commanded, a force that could reduce a thousand years of Geomancer history to a fine, black dust. He had watched both Geomancers and vampires fall before him, their ancient pride crumbling in the face of a single, terrible storm.

But he knew this was not the end.

He was not a son who had become a monster. He was a monster who had become a Lunar Geomancer, and that distinction mattered. Power had carried him this far, but survival in the world that remained would demand more. The Geomancers might be broken, the vampires scattered, yet the werewolves still prowled, and the humans—cunning, ambitious, and desperate—would never hesitate to chain or use him if they could.

He needed more. Not just strength, but mastery. Not just destruction, but dominion.

He turned his back on the Sanctum, its once-proud halls reduced to silence and dust. It was no longer his prison, nor his home. He would not return until he came as more than a survivor or an avenger. He would return as a king.

His prey was no longer living enemies, but power itself. He would hunt the relics of the Geomancers—the scrolls, the stones, the forbidden texts that even the elders had feared to touch. He would seek out the artifacts of the vampires—the blood of the Ancients, the bones of old kings, the secrets of immortality. He would even seek the lore of the werewolves, the primal truths whispered only under moonlight. He would not simply defeat his enemies. He would become them. Their secrets, their strengths, their fears—he would claim them all.

And so the hunt began.

At the heart of the ruins, the shattered wards of the Sanctum began to stir. Their cracks deepened, their protections faltered, but not by accident. Faustus had left behind a mark of himself—a pulse of raw, untamed Geomancy deliberately broadcast into the dark world. A beacon. A challenge.

To those who still hunted him, it was an irresistible call. To those who sought him, it was an invitation. And to those who feared him, it was a warning.

The world would hear the call of a king.

The Beacon of Power

The pulse of Faustus's Geomancy rippled far beyond the ruins of the Sanctum. It was not a whisper but a roar, a low, steady thrum that bled into the soil, into the rivers, into the marrow of the world. For those attuned to power, it was impossible to ignore.

The Wolves: Deep in the forests, Glavius felt it first. To him, it was not terror but promise. The others cowered at the thought of the Lunar Geomancer, but Glavius heard in that pulse the rhythm of his own ambition. The boy was not to be feared. He was to be claimed. The pack had been hunters of deer and men; now they would become hunters of kings.

The Vampires: Scattered remnants of Lord Elden's army clawed their way out of the dust and fire of Faustus's storm. Their lord had vanished into the shadows, but his whispers lingered like poison in their veins: *Survive. Wait. Watch.* When the beacon struck them, their instincts recoiled in fear, but their hunger pulled them forward. If they could not conquer this power, perhaps they could bleed it, drink it, twist it into their own.

The Humans: Even among the Geomancer survivors Bella had gathered, the beacon stirred unease. They whispered that Faustus had not fled but was calling challengers, daring the world to come. Some spoke of prophecy, others of doom, but all agreed: a storm had been loosed, and none could hide from its call.

A World in Motion

The result was not immediate armies marching, but currents shifting:

Glavius rallies his new Alpha faction, convinced that destiny lies in binding Faustus to the wolves.

Vampire agents scatter like shadows, intent on tracking the source of the pulse before it grows beyond their reach.

Bella and Bryn, already following their son's trail, now find themselves racing not just to reach him—but to reach him before anyone else does.

CHAPTER FORTY-NINE

THE NEW SANCTUM

REBUILDING

Years had slipped past like frost from a morning stone.

The Sanctum, once a cold geometry of power and punishment, rose again under gentler hands. Bella stood in the central court where shards had once sung with ruin. Now the stone breathed. Under her touch, broken lintels knit without a scar; walls re-grew from rubble in layered veins of granite and clay; the last intact Heartstones shed their harsh glare and settled into a low, protective hum. She worked slowly, stubbornly, as if each repaired seam might stitch shut a wound memory could not.

Her hair had threaded with silver. The thin, pale ridge of the scar along her cheek no longer felt like a brand but a boundary—of what she had survived, and what she would not allow to return.

Children's voices—careful, hushed at first—echoed through the colonnades. The spared and the strayed: junior mages, archivists, ward-runners who had obeyed orders because they'd never been allowed a choice. Bella taught them to listen before they shaped, to ask the earth for its angle and weight, to use power like a promise rather than a blade. Stones moved for them when they spoke kindly; water came sweet from the cistern when they thanked it. Those who had only known discipline learned craft. Those who had only known fear learned purpose.

Bryn became the Sanctum's silhouette.

He ranged the tree line at dusk and returned at dawn, smoke and pine tangled in his hair. He hunted, patched roofs, pulled down the charred bones of old scaffolds, and drove iron pegs into new. He spoke little. Sometimes in evening's blue hour, Bella would find him seated on the parapet with his back to the rebuilt wards, gaze on the far ridges as if listening for footsteps that would never come. Orin's. Emor's. The pack's. He did not say their names. Grief was a labor he did with his hands.

Between them lay a faithful quiet—shared pots, shared tools, shared watch—but not yet a shared truth. The lie she carried for their son had settled into her body the way a thorn settles beneath skin: the flesh grows around it; the pain dulls; the harm remains. She could not give it voice. To speak it would be to break him and break what these new children had begun here: lessons at sunrise, bread at noon, laughter in the cloister when a practice arch held its curve.

Sometimes, by the fire, she let memory speak instead.

"He was not weak," she said once, while ember light wrote restless copper in Bryn's eyes. "Your brother."

Bryn's mouth tightened. "He mistook mercy for strength."

"He knew mercy is how strength doesn't turn to rot," she answered. "He died choosing love when cruelty was easier." Her thumb grazed the rim of a clay cup. "That is a kind of courage even the earth remembers."

Bryn looked back to the ridges. He didn't argue. He did not agree. He only sat with the words like a wound he refused to reopen and could not close.

Faustus did not walk the halls, but he was present in them—an after-swell in the mortar, a lunar pressure in the glass. The Sanctum's new wards held, mercifully; his resonance passed through like distant weather, felt more than heard. When Bella paused with her palms on warm stone, she could sense the direction of him: not a scream now, not even a demand—just a vector. Moving. Gathering. Learning what the old world had hoarded and how to prise it loose.

She rebuilt anyway. You do not stop laying a foundation because the sky darkens. You place another stone and make sure the children stand beneath an arch.

Retreat

Beyond the river, something older than stone licked its wounds.

Lord Elden watched the far valley from a ruinous belfry where owls nested in the ribs of a bell. He had learned to be still even when the night felt thin. Once, he had been a neat solution to chaos; now, he was an equation with too many unknowns. He had no legions left to polish the silence behind him. Dust had a way of humbling architects.

Retreat was not cowardice; it was math. You hide to draw lines between what you want and what you can survive. He sent the remnants of his court into the earth like seeds into a fallow field. They would not starve. They would listen. They would let rumor do its work, and rot, and time. And if the boy's blaze burned hottest early—as great fires sometimes do—there might come a season for a careful hand to shape the ash.

For now, he chose patience. Hunger could be stored like coin.

Rebirth

The Sanctum learned a new rhythm: mortar, lesson, watch; bread, lesson, watch. At dusk, the children chalked slow circles and whispered thanks; at dawn, the gardens returned small green proofs that the earth forgave what it could. Bella taught names for stone that were not spells: bedding plane, fieldstone, weight. She taught a boy to listen for the seam before he set the wedge; she taught a girl to shore the narrow wall with a laugh, because fear shakes a hand and laughter steadies it.

One night on the parapet, Bryn found her tracing the ward-script with two fingers, like a mother counting a sleeping child's breaths.

"He will come back," he said, not as prophecy, not as threat. A simple fact with nowhere to sit.

"I know," she answered. Her voice held neither panic nor relief—only readiness. "We'll have a door for him. And rules inside it."

"We may need a wall," Bryn said.

"We have one," she said, looking over the courtyard where lamplight made islands of the new. "We didn't build it to keep him out."

He fell quiet. The wind plucked at the ward-flags. Somewhere below, a child laughed in their sleep.

His Return

When the moon hung thin and white, Bella rose before dawn and ran her palm along the stones she'd set the day before, as if reading a book into which she had written herself. She could have shaped the world harder, faster; that was a truth she kept as guarded as any secret. But the Sanctum must not learn fear of her. Power turned to fear is an old story with a hundred endings and only one grief.

So, she built slowly. So, she taught gently. So, she kept the thorn unspoken.

And if at times her hand strayed to the scar on her cheek and stayed there, at times the memories of painful love scarred again under her touch like a heartbeat finding its measure—no one mentioned it. Even stone understands the language of a quiet promise.

The Sanctum endured. It breathed. It waited.

And far off, where the sky looked thinner, a boy they loved and feared took steps they could not hear.

CHAPTER FIFTY

THE LAST VAMPIRES

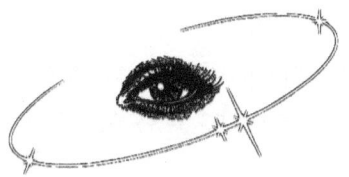

DUST AND TERROR

The fine, black dust of a thousand souls was all that remained of Lord Elden's proud army. He stood on a high hill, his pale face, a mask carved from sorrow and centuries of undeath. His amber eyes, which had watched empires rise and crumble, now burned with something far more corrosive than rage: a cold, unyielding terror.

Never, in a thousand years of conquest, had he seen a power like this. The Geomancers' Sanctum—once a glittering prize to be claimed—was now a grave. The boy they had called a weapon was no longer a child. Faustus was a Lunar Geomancer, and he had become a force of nature.

Behind Elden huddled his surviving lieutenants, no more than ten. They had survived by chance, clinging to the farthest shadows of the battlefield while their brothers and sisters had been turned to ash. They looked at the scorched field below, their fear thick enough to taste. The world had changed, and they knew it: vampires were no longer the hunters. They were prey.

"We retreat," Elden said, his voice stripped of grandeur, leaving only gravel and command. No vengeance, no talk of conquest—only survival.

A Predator's Game

Their flight through the forest was desperate, graceless. They did not glide like shadows of the night; they ran, hunted things scattering in panic.

But the chase was never about speed. Faustus did not track them with scent or sound. He stalked them with presence. His power, a steady thrum of lunar Geomancy, pressed against their minds like a storm cloud swollen with lightning.

He did not rush to finish them. He toyed with them, cruel as a cat with a mouse. He wanted them to feel his closeness, his inevitability.

When the first scream split the night, it belonged to a young hunter who collapsed clutching his skull. The ground beneath him convulsed, roots snapping like whips. In a breath, he was gone—swept into a blur of stone and fire, leaving nothing but dust.

The others froze in horror. They could not outrun what moved the earth itself.

The Council of the Ancients

The psychic wave of Faustus's destruction rippled across the world, striking even the distant vampire courts. Within marble halls lit by black flame, the Ancients gathered—a conclave of predators who had once believed themselves eternal.

Lord Elden stumbled into their midst, hollowed by defeat. He spoke of the Sanctum reduced to ash, of the army erased, of the boy who had become storm and judgment. His words fell heavy into silence.

Count Arad, oldest among them, rose from his throne of obsidian. His tall, gaunt frame radiated authority, his amber eyes hard with resolve.

"The child is no longer a weapon," he declared, his voice like the crack of stone. "He is a force of nature. We will not chase vengeance. We will not repeat Elden's folly. We will endure, we will unite, and we will build an army unlike the world has ever seen. Not to contain him—but to erase him."

The court stirred, not with hunger but with fear turned to iron resolve. A new war was forming—one of survival.

The Girl with Bella's Eyes

Faustus entered the ruined temple like a shadow given form. His steps made no sound, but the earth itself trembled beneath the pressure of his will. The air was thick with ash and dread, the scent of blood and centuries of undeath clinging to every stone. Five vampires huddled together, their pale faces caught in the faint light that bled through the broken roof.

The ground split at his gesture, swallowing three in a violent cascade of stone and fire. They vanished without even a scream, reduced to dust in the space between breaths. Only two remained: an elder, brittle and slow, his resignation written across his hollow face—and a girl.

She was young, newly turned. Unlike the others, her flesh still held the warmth of recent life. Her long black hair spilled like ink across her shoulders, and her eyes—blue, impossibly blue—pierced him like a memory. Bella's eyes. His mother's eyes.

The ground stilled. His power faltered.

The elder shrank back, whimpering prayers to forgotten gods, but the girl did not move. She stood in the ruin as if it were her birthright, her hands empty, her body trembling—but her gaze steady. She did not scream. She did not beg. She looked at him as if she had already measured the weight of her death and accepted it.

"My lord," she whispered. Her voice was soft, musical, but it carried through the silence like a blade. "We are not a threat. We are all that is left. Please... spare us."

Something inside Faustus twisted. Rage, always his constant companion, found itself smothered by something heavier: memory. Her eyes were different. Her laugh. Her touch reminded him of the love he once felt. The way he had once felt, like the center of her world, before the lies, before the unborn sibling who had stolen his love.

His breath came ragged, the power thrumming through him surging and recoiling in equal measure. This girl—this vampire—looked at him not as a monster, but as a son. As a wounded child.

"Who are you?" he asked, the words breaking from him like a confession. His voice was not the guttural rumble of the Lunar Geomancer who had destroyed armies—it was the voice of a boy lost in the ruins of himself.

She bowed her head slightly, not in submission, but in quiet respect. "My name is Seraphina. Seraphina Lacroix. I was a scholar before the turning. I am no warrior, no leader. I only remember. I witness. I write. That is my purpose." She lifted her gaze again, steady and unflinching. "If you kill me, I will be forgotten. But if you let me live, I will carry your story. I will remember you as more than vengeance."

The words struck deeper than any blade. No one had ever spoken to him that way—not the Geomancers who had caged him, not the wolves who hunted him, not even Bella, whose silence had been its own betrayal. Seraphina's voice was a fragile bridge over the abyss in his heart, and for one fleeting instant, he let himself stand upon it.

The elder vampire whimpered again, breaking the moment. Faustus's eyes snapped toward him, and with a flick of his hand, the old one was gone—consumed by the earth, dust on the wind. But Seraphina remained.

The torrent of Geomancy faded, leaving only silence, heavy and suffocating. For the first time since his rise, Faustus spared a life. Not out of mercy. Not out of weakness. But because in Seraphina, he saw something he could not destroy: the memory of his mother's love, and the possibility—however fragile—that he was not doomed to be a monster alone.

Arad's Plan

Among the dust and terror of the collapsing vampire strongholds, Seraphina remained at Faustus's side. Her beauty was striking, but it carried an unsettling familiarity—the curve of her cheek, the midnight black of her hair, the eyes that mirrored deep waters. She was not Bella, yet in the torchlight, she *echoed* her. Enough to stir old ghosts in Faustus's heart.

It had not been chance. Count Arad had chosen her for that purpose. In the centuries when his power still commanded loyalty, he had plucked Seraphina from obscurity and bound her to vampirism, not for her strength or cunning, but for her resemblance to the woman Faustus had once whispered of in his madness. Arad believed that memory could be weaponized, that desire could tether even a cursed acolyte.

And so Seraphina was fashioned into an enchantment—a living snare wearing the mask of lost love. She knew it. Arad had told her plainly: "Your face will break him or bind him. Either way, he will be mine."

But time and ruin had twisted the plan. Faustus, haunted and hollow, saw in her not merely Bella's likeness but something else—a chance at absolution. Where Arad intended chains, Faustus found the faintest illusion of freedom. He listened to Seraphina's voice, softer than the Count's commands, and for the first time since the book had consumed him, he felt seen.

Seraphina, for her part, had been a pawn too long. She learned to wield her resemblance not as a curse but as leverage, pressing against the cracks in Faustus's armor. In their stolen silences, she asked him not of conquest, but of memory:

"What was she like?"

"Did you love her before the world burned?"

His answers came haltingly, pieces of a past buried in ash. And though Seraphina had been made in Bella's shadow, she began to carve her own shape in Faustus's heart. Not the same. Never the same. But something that unsettled the ghosts Count Arad had intended to chain him with.

When the armies of the Sanctum closed in and the vampire courts fell to dust, Seraphina stood beside Faustus not as Arad's lure, but as her own. In her, he saw both the cruelty of Arad's manipulations and the possibility of something the world had long denied him: a choice not born of fear or duty, but of fragile, dangerous affection.

And though the night belonged to ruin, the bond forged in deception and reshaped in defiance would not be so easily scattered with the ashes.

CHAPTER FIFTY-ONE

THE RETURN OF THE SON

A SON'S SURPRISE

T he Sanctum, rebuilt by Bella's hands, stood as a fortress of stone and light. Its gates, once the proud doors of a cold order, were now meant as symbols of hope. But hope was fragile, and Bella knew it.

The night before, she had dreamt of loss again. This time, it was not the faceless wolf tearing at her womb, but Faustus himself. He stood where her child once had, cold and merciless, and she awoke gasping — sweat slick on her skin, her hands trembling against an emptiness she knew too well. The unease followed her all day, clinging like a shadow.

And then he came.

Faustus and Seraphina appeared at the Sanctum's gates, a dark silhouette beside a pale one. Faustus's deep blue eyes glowed faintly, his presence heavy and exacting, as if the stones themselves bent to him.

Seraphina, with her fair skin and sapphire eyes, seemed a haunting echo of Bella's younger self — familiar enough to unmoor her, strange enough to terrify her.

They were not family. They were two broken beings, carrying with them the promise of war.

The gates creaked open. Bella and Bryn stepped forward. She was pale, her lips parted in disbelief. Bryn was rigid, a sentinel braced for a blow. Faustus's gaze locked on them, unreadable, while Seraphina lingered half a step behind, her stillness unnatural, her presence unsettling.

"Faustus..." Bella whispered, her voice trembling. "We can talk. We can be a family again."

Faustus laughed — a hollow, empty sound that chilled the courtyard. "Family?" he said, the word twisted with disdain.

His eyes shifted to Bryn. "Pathetic. After everything... you remain with her."

Bryn stiffened, but said nothing. Faustus's face turned back to Bella — and for an instant, something faltered. The cold gleam in his eyes wavered, replaced by something raw, almost desperate. The way he had looked at her once as a child.

That moment was shattered by Bryn's voice. "Son," he said quietly, his tone edged with urgency. "Your mother loves you. She would do anything for you. Stay. Help us build something better — a world worth living in. One you can be proud of."

Faustus tilted his head toward Bryn, his stare sharp, cruel. For a heartbeat, he seemed less a son and more a predator sizing up prey.

Then his voice came, low and gravelly. "Tell me, mother. How can you stand with him after what happened? After *his* failure cost you your child?"

Bryn blinked, confused. "What child?" he asked, his voice unsteady. "What are you talking about? What did I do?"

Faustus's cold laughter returned, sharper now. "The child that lived in her womb. The one you failed to protect. The one I chose to let die."

The words cut deeper than any blade. Bella staggered back as if struck. The secret she had carried for so long — a lie built from grief, silence, and survival — was torn into the open by her own son.

Bryn turned to her slowly. His face, usually a mask of stern resolve, was stripped bare, raw with disbelief. In her silence, he found only confirmation.

Faustus watched it all with a terrible stillness. He felt her grief — a wave that struck him harder than his own fury. She had sacrificed *his sibling*. For Bryn. For a man not his father. The thought seared him like fire.

"You lied to me," he said, his voice breaking with venom. "You made me your weapon. You made me your monster." His power trembled around him — a faint quake in the stones, a hush in the wind — but he did not unleash it. Not yet.

The courtyard, meant as a sanctuary, had become a stage for betrayal. Bella could not meet Bryn's eyes. Bryn could not understand her silence. And Faustus, with Seraphina at his side, stood as both judge and executioner.

But no blow fell. Only silence did.

Faustus lowered his gaze, his expression unreadable, and whispered one last word that echoed in the hollow chamber of their hearts:

"Liars."

And then he turned away, leaving them in the ruin of their own truth.

Interlude: The Weight of Silence

The courtyard of the Sanctum, where Faustus's words had shattered the fragile bond of family, lay wrapped in silence. The fire-pits had long since gone cold, their ashes scattering like the remnants of trust. The stones seemed to hold their breath, as though even the earth recoiled from what had been spoken.

Bella sat alone in the shadows of the gate, her body still, but her mind a torrent. She held herself as though clutching her own ribs was the only way to keep from breaking apart completely. Every glance toward Bryn stabbed deeper — the man she loved, the man she had lied to. She could not meet his eyes, for in them she would see not fury, but worse: the hollow void of betrayal.

Bryn stood apart, his back turned to her, a sentinel carved from grief. He did not speak, because there were no words. The silence was his shield, the only barrier between himself and a truth too raw to face. He replayed Faustus's words again and again, each repetition a blade twisting deeper. A child? A secret buried in sorrow? His mind was a battlefield of disbelief and despair.

Above them, the Sanctum's rebuilt walls groaned softly in the night wind, as though mourning alongside its keepers. Seraphina lingered in the doorway, silent as a shadow, watching. She alone spoke no words, and yet her presence was a reminder: this fracture was not just between mother and father, but a wound that might echo across worlds.

Days blurred into one another. They ate in silence, slept in silence, moved through the Sanctum like phantoms of their former selves. Words hovered on Bella's lips each night but never escaped. Bryn's gaze lingered on her too long, but his mouth never asked the questions that clawed inside him.

And so the silence became their prison — heavier than any chain, sharper than any blade, a silence that promised to consume them both if it held much longer.

CHAPTER FIFTY-TWO

AN EYE FOR AN EYE

A VOW OF BLOOD AND BONE

T he words — jagged shards of truth — did not surprise Bryn. They merely confirmed what his heart had long feared. His mate, his love, had lost a child. His son, his monster, had allowed it to happen. And now, in the same breath, he had learned he was to be a father once more. But what he found at the Sanctum was not life. It was a grave. Not family. A lie.

Shock gripped him first, cold and suffocating. But grief is never still. It twisted, hardened, ignited. A fire roared through him — not the tempered fire of a warrior, but the blind, searing blaze of a wolf undone. He turned, his gaze fixed not on Faustus, but on Seraphina.

Her hand rested protectively on her belly, her other hand trembling at her side. The scent was undeniable, a whisper of life, of blood and bone yet to be born. His instincts screamed the truth: another VonPelt pup stirred within her. His mind spun back to the moment Bella had been attacked, the inexplicable absence of Faustus's protection, the gaps in her story. I was a fool for refusing to see it. A coward for not confronting her. Now, every missing piece slammed into place with cruel finality.

Bryn no longer saw Seraphina. He saw the grave of his unborn child. He saw betrayal given form. He saw the cruel mockery of legacy. A guttural snarl tore free, half sob, half scream. He lunged.

Seraphina's sapphire eyes widened — not with the arrogance of an elder vampire, but with the primal terror of a mother-to-be. She raised her hands, but Bryn's fury was swifter, heavier, final. The courtyard swallowed her scream, and then there was only silence. Her gaze, full of heartbreak and finality, fixed on Faustus. Then faded.

The faint hum of unborn life, so fragile yet so luminous, blinked out like a candle in storm. Faustus froze. For an instant, he was not a Lunar Geomancer, not vengeance made flesh — he was a boy again. A boy losing everything in the space of a breath. And then the boy was gone. In his place stood fury incarnate. His eyes flared, blue light bleeding into the dark like fire spilling from a wound.

Bryn turned, claws still dripping, toward his son. His face was a mask carved from pain and resolve, but his intent was clear: one death was not enough.

"Bryn!" Bella's scream cut through the courtyard like glass breaking. "Stop! Please, stop!" Her voice cracked, thick with terror. She saw them both for what they were: wolves of blood and bone, bound not by love but by vengeance, ready to devour one another.

Faustus's silence was more terrible than any roar. He raised his hand, Lunar power gathering, raw and infinite. The air itself bent around him, a storm waiting for release. Bryn crouched, ready to strike again. His claws gleamed, his breath ragged, his eyes locked on his son.

The vow was unspoken but etched in their blood: one of them would not leave this place alive.

A Family Conflict

The courtyard was silent, every stone a witness to the breaking of a family. Bryn stood trembling, his grief sharpened into feral rage. His body was a scarred monument of hunts and losses, but his eyes burned with the raw fury of a father betrayed. Opposite him, Faustus stood unshaken — a cold pillar of lunar light. His deep blue eyes glowed faintly, not with warmth, but with the distant, unyielding brilliance of a force no longer human. Bella's scream cut through the stillness.

"Faustus! Stop! Please, stop!" She was crumpled on the stone floor, her hands pressed to her chest as if trying to hold her breaking heart together. She saw the truth neither man could deny: Bryn was no match for their son. Faustus was no child — he was a Lunar Geomancer; a storm wrapped in flesh.

The first clash came like lightning. Bryn lunged, silver-tipped blade flashing. He was speed, fury, instinct. But Faustus did not move. He merely raised a hand. The earth itself revolted.

Roots tore free, stone split apart, and a blast of raw Geomancy hurled Bryn backward like a rag doll. He hit the courtyard wall with a sickening crack, blood staining the ancient stone. Still, he rose — battered, broken, but defiant. Faustus watched with chilling detachment. He had no intention of ending it quickly. He wanted Bryn to feel the hollow pain of loss, the suffocating fire of grief. He wanted him to suffer. The air thickened, shimmering with the hum of gathering power, as if the Sanctum itself held its breath.

"Faustus!" Bella cried again, crawling forward, her voice breaking. "He is your father! He is your family!"

For a moment — a heartbeat — the words pierced him. The cold mask of vengeance faltered, and in Faustus's eyes a flicker of sorrow threatened to surface. Bryn, crumpled and gasping, lifted his gaze, no longer full of rage but of desperate love. And then the moment shattered.

Faustus's hand clenched. The ground trembled. With a brutal, final gesture, he tore the earth open beneath Bryn's feet. The wolf fell into the yawning abyss, swallowed whole by shadow and stone.

The Sanctum — rebuilt as a refuge of hope — became a tomb.

Bella's scream echoed against the ruined walls, raw and primal, carrying the weight of every loss she had endured. And Faustus, standing over the chasm, was not a son anymore. He was a Lunar Geomancer, a storm in human form, and his terrible choice had ended the war for their family.

CHAPTER FIFTY-THREE

THE SEISMIC SHIFT

FACTIONS

The world groaned as though some ancient truth had been broken. From the heart of the Sanctum, Faustus's fury had cracked stone and split soil, but what followed was deeper still. A tremor of power spread outward, not in violent waves but in a slow, rolling silence that unsettled everything it touched.

The Wolves

Far in the forests, the pack stirred uneasily. The earth whispered beneath their paws, not in quakes but in heartbeats. Some pressed themselves to the ground, whining, unable to endure the resonance. Their Alpha spoke no words; his silence was more frightening than any growl. In that stillness, every wolf knew: something greater than their blood had awakened.

The Vampires

In a distant citadel, goblets of crimson stilled mid-ripple. Candles guttered and died without wind. The ancients, lords of shadow and eternity, froze in their halls. No speeches were made, no threats issued. Their silence was colder than their crypts. For the first time in centuries, the dead remembered fear.

The Geomancers

Scattered survivors clutched their stones and wards, only to find them dull and lifeless. The power that had once been their refuge was muted, as if the earth itself no longer answered their call. They did not speak. They dared not. For the silence told them more than words: their world had been claimed by another.

The Mortals

In villages where no name of Faustus had ever been spoken, children woke weeping, their dreams full of cracking stone and a pale blue fire. Dogs barked at nothing until their throats went raw. Old priests marked circles in ash and whispered prayers to gods who did not answer. Farmers stared at their fields, sensing that the ground they tilled no longer belonged to them.

In the Sanctum

Bella's sobs were the only human sound against the hollow echo of stone. Bryn's absence was still settling into the air, like smoke after a fire. Faustus stood unmoving, his eyes a blue flame without warmth, while the tremor he had unleashed crawled farther across the world.

The seismic shift was not a single event. It was a sentence, carried on the bones of the earth:

The age of balance had ended. A new dominion was awakening.

CHAPTER FIFTY-FOUR

THE FINAL ACT

PUTTING A HALT

T he courtyard was silent, save for the moan of wind through broken stone. The ground was still a raw, gaping wound where Bryn had been swallowed. Bella lay on the cold floor, her body trembling, her eyes fixed on the abyss that had taken her love. She was no Geomancer in that moment. No warrior. Only a mother staring at the ruin her son had wrought.

Faustus stood above her, framed by storm light. His deep blue eyes—no longer eyes of a boy, but the cold, unfeeling lanterns of a Lunar Geomancer—glowed with a terrible certainty. He did not cry. He did not tremble. He only raised his hands, and the storm bent to him. Lightning danced at his fingertips. Thunder rolled in his chest. The very air became his weapon.

A house across the courtyard caught his attention, a humble place where a widowed mage sheltered his three children. Faustus's gaze hardened. Bella followed it, her blood freezing as realization struck.

"Faustus—STOP!" she cried.

But the plea was drowned in flame. The red light in his hands burst forth, and the small home incinerated in a scream of fire. A man's silhouette stumbled into the courtyard, clutching three small shapes, all of them aflame. They collapsed in a heap of ash and bone before Bella's horrified eyes. She smothered the fire with her own power, but by then, nothing living remained.

An old man peered from a nearby doorway, too slow to hide again. Faustus turned toward him with a cruel laugh.
"Cold, old man? Shall I warm you?"

A snap of his hand. The elder burst into fire, gone in seconds, reduced to dust carried on the storm.

Bella's breath caught in her chest. This thing—her son, her flesh—was nothing but a monster now. The protector she had once prayed for was lost to her forever.

Faustus lifted both hands. Lightning coiled into his palms, swelling into a final, annihilating storm meant for the Sanctum itself. His storm was absolute, his power unstoppable. But Bella still moved.

Her shield rose in an instant—light, stone, and will interweave into one unbreakable wall. Faustus's strike slammed into it, only to whip back with violent force. The backlash hurled him across the courtyard. His body crashed into stone, sliding down in a heap. For the first time in all his years of battle, Faustus had fallen. He did not land on his feet.

He rose slowly; his eyes locked on his mother. And in her face he saw not sorrow, not weakness—but fury. A cold, unyielding fury that mirrored his own. Bella's expression froze him. She had never frowned in anger before, never turned her grief into something so sharp and merciless. In that moment, Faustus—the predator, the Alpha, the self-proclaimed god—knew fear.

Step by step, he backed away, unwilling to expose his throat. He left not in defeat, but in retreat, his storm receding into silence.

Bella stood in the ruins, her shield dissolving into ash. She knew she could have ended it, could have cleansed the world of its terror with one blow. But her heart had faltered. Faustus was her child. No matter how monstrous, no matter how far he had fallen, the bond was unbreakable.

And yet, the flame of her love was dim. A candle, flickering in the storm. Fading—but still lit. And sometimes, in a world as broken as theirs, a single flame was enough to keep the night at bay.

CHAPTER FIFTY-FIVE

EMBERS AND SHADOWS

EMPTINESS IN THE SANCTUM

The Sanctum was quiet again, but it was not peace. The storm had passed, leaving broken stone and shattered lives in its wake. Bella walked through the ruins with slow, deliberate steps, her hand trailing across the walls she had once rebuilt. Her heart felt as hollow as the halls, yet she could not falter. Survivors looked to her, their faces pale with fear, their eyes asking questions she could not answer.

She gathered them in the central courtyard. With trembling hands, she lit a single candle on the altar of stone. Its glow was faint, fragile, but it was light. She told them they would rebuild, again. That the Sanctum would stand, not as a weapon, but as a refuge. Yet as the candle flickered, she knew the truth—the fire was all that remained of her love for her son. Still lit, but fragile. One breath away from darkness.

Far beyond the Sanctum, Faustus moved through a desolate forest. His steps were steady, but inside, his fury boiled. His mother had humbled him, forced him to the ground, and the image of her unflinching face haunted him more than the defeat itself. For the first time, he had felt fear—not of death, but of her.

At the edge of a blackened lake, he paused. In his hands he held a shard of obsidian, humming with an ancient resonance. The storm within him poured into the stone, and it glowed faintly red, alive with his rage. He did not look back toward the Sanctum. He would not return until he could bend the world itself to his will. Until the flame in his mother's heart was extinguished.

Bella stood in the Sanctum's highest tower, watching the horizon. She could not see him, but she felt him—a presence tethered to her soul, moving farther away yet growing stronger with every step.

Faustus, at the black lake, closed his fist around the shard. In the reflection of the water, his deep blue eyes gleamed with lunar fire.

Mother and son, bound by blood and betrayal, stood on opposite ends of a world that could not contain them both. One lit a fragile candle of hope. The other carried a stone of vengeance.

The story was not over. It had only begun.

EPILOGUE

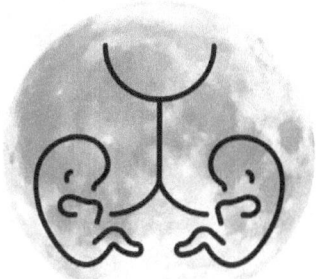

THE FIRST CRY

T he world had narrowed to a single, white-hot point of pain. Each push was a tearing, primal act, every breath edged with ash and fire. The midwife's voice guided her, though the words blurred into nothing but rhythm. All that mattered was the struggle—the will to bring life into a world already drowning in death.

Then—release. A cry split the silence, low and guttural at first, almost a growl, before softening into the fragile wail of a newborn. The midwife gasped.

Placed upon her chest, the child was not what she expected. Thick, dark hair crowned its head and traced down its shoulders like a living pelt. Tiny fists clenched, and the same coarse growth bristled along the knuckles.

The baby drew another breath, and the sound was older than its minutes on this earth—an animal rumble before the human cry followed.

But before wonder could take root, pain seized her again. The second came faster, as if impatient to arrive. Smaller, yet born the same: a strange coat of shadowed hair, a twin bound by the same uncanny mark.

Laid together, their cries wove into something more unsettling. One snarled, a sharp, toothless mimicry of a predator. The other whimpered, fragile but insistent. Two halves of a song that seemed to echo from some older, darker age.

The midwife, pale, whispered in horror: *"Twins...again."*

The woman did not answer. Whether her silence was from shock, exhaustion, or a vow she dared not speak, none could tell. She only gathered them into her arms, holding the strange infants close against her breast. Her eyes glistened—not with fear, but with a fierce, primal love.

Above them, moonlight slashed through a crack in the roof, silver and merciless. It lit their furred backs, their writhing little bodies, as their sounds filled the chamber—growl and cry, predator and child, ancient and new.

BELLA: CHILDREN OF THE MOON - A FREE PREVIEW

A QUIET CONSPIRACY

The world still trembled from the Reckoning's echoes.

Smoke drifted above a ruined village, its hearths long cold, its walls broken and silent.

Two figures lingered among the rubble.

Elder Myr, his face a mask of patient cruelty, traced a clawlike hand across a shattered stone. Beside him stood Jorric, his bulk shadowing the moonlight, his jaw set with barely contained fury.

"It worked," Myr said, his tone like parchment crumbling. "Orin and the girl—woven together, as I planned. Blood, desire, ruin. The cycle always yields what I need."

Jorric's lip curled. "And yet ruin breeds heirs. Faustus walks the earth, and whispers now speak of... twins."

Myr's eyes, black wells of malice, gleamed. "Yes. Again, the blood repeats itself. Again, the world forgets its lesson. But I do not forget. Blood is a tool. And if I shape the blood, I shape the future."

Far in the night, faint as a ghost, came the echo of two cries—one soft and whimpering, the other low, almost a growl.

Jorric spat into the dirt. "Another curse. Another doom."

"No," Myr whispered, his voice sharp as broken glass. "Another chance. Another game."

The moonlight cut across the ruins, silver and merciless, as the two men vanished into the dark.

And in their wake lingered only a promise—one that the world, already bleeding, was too blind to see.

ABOUT THE AUTHOR

Rick Sanchez is a registered nurse with over fourteen years of experience in healthcare, where compassion, resilience, and endurance have been at the heart of every day. Beyond the hospital walls, creativity has always been a constant companion. From years spent as a barista perfecting the art of craft and connection, to exploring graphic design and other artistic pursuits, storytelling has always lingered in the background, waiting for its moment.

That moment has arrived with *Bella: Cursed World – Forbidden Love*, Rick's debut fantasy novel. Blending a love of myth, dark romance, and richly built worlds, this first book marks the beginning of a new creative chapter.

When not writing or working in nursing, Rick explores a wide range of passions: photography, home beer making, cooking, and cocktail crafting. Whether behind a camera lens or at the kitchen counter, creativity shapes every part of life. And while nursing may be a profession, art remains the heartbeat that carries through every endeavor.

CHARACTER NAMES

P ronounciations

Bella Lestaire: BEH-luh *leh-STAIR*
Loryndor: 'LOR-in-dor
Orin VonPelt: OR-in *von-PELT*
Bryn: BRIHN
Emor: 'EE-mor
Faustus: *'FAW-stus*
Faust Modaine: FAWST Moh-dayn
Jorric Boyd: 'JOR-ik *BOYD*
Franc: FRAHNK
Myr Straus: MEER *STROWSS*
Delani Crane: Deh-LAH-nee Krayn
Magistra Lycah Bellevue: 'MAG-ih-strah *'LEE-kah BELL-vyoo*
Seraphina Lacroix: SEHR-uh-'FEE-nuh *luh-KR WAH*
Glavius Lynch: 'GLAY-vee-us *LINCH*
Jina: Jee-nah
Mora: Mor-ah
Jasper: JAS-per
Arad DeLavoit: 'AH-rad *deh-lah-VWAH*
Myk Yonder: MIKE *YON-der*
Terrek Greybeard: TERR-ek GRAY-beerd
Vlad Karlov: Vlahd Kar-lov

Ian Grok: EE-an Grahk

Griseld Pitt: GRIH-seld PIT

Elden Ferrow: 'EL-den FAIR-oh

Veyla: VAY-luh

Thalos: *THAH-lohs*

Rosianna Holt: *ROH-zee-AH-nuh* HOHLT

Heartstone: 'HART-stohn

Sanctum: 'SANK-tum

Lunar Geomancer: 'LOO-nar 'JEE-oh-man-ser

www.ingramcontent.com/pod-product-compliance
Lightning Source LLC
Chambersburg PA
CBHW030423180626
46812CB00005B/2150